BLOOD CURSE

ALSO BY T. G. AYER

Young Adult Paranormal

THE VALKYRIE SERIES

Dead Radiance

Dead Radiance Audio

Dead Embers

Dead Embers Audio

Dead Chaos

Dead Chaos Audio

Dead Wrath

Dead Silence

Joshua - Dead Radiance

Joshua II - Dead Embers

Joshua III - Dead Chaos

Joshua IV - Dead Wrath

Joshua V - Dead Silence

THE HAND OF KALI SERIES

Fire & Shadow

Blood & Gold

Time & Fate

Fury & Virtue

Spirit & Soul

THE DARKWORLD ORIGINS

Pyros (Logan)
Ailuros (Kailin)

~

THE DARK SIGHT SERIES

Dark Sight
Cursed Sight
Vissarion
Shadow Sight
Dark Prophecy
Cursed Prophecy
Shadow Prophecy

~

THE APSARA CHRONICLES

Immortal Bound
Gods Ascendent
Dominion Falling
Vengeance Born
Last Legion

~

A SEASON OF ASH AND BONE

Heartfyre

~

Adult Sci-Fi

HANDS ASSASSIN

Death Dealer

Death Mark

Death Strike

Hand's Assassins Series

~

NEW ADULT CONTEMPORARY THRILLER W/A TONI VALLAN

Beautiful Collision

Beautiful Conviction

~

PSYCHOLOGICAL HORROR W/A TONI VALLAN

Dark Shadows

Splinter

BLOOD CURSE

THE SOULTRACKER SERIES 3

Cover art by Eduardo Priego

ISBN-13: 978-0995112513

BLOOD CURSE

USA TODAY BESTSELLING AUTHOR

T.G. AYER

The truth is, pretending everything is okay can get a girl in far more trouble than actually admitting that shit is going seriously wrong.

How can anything be okay when I know my sister is alive but I have no idea where she is, or how it's even possible for her to *be* alive?

How can anything be okay when my head pounds every second of the day, when every morning my pillow is streaked red and I can't tell if the blood came from my nose, or my ears, or my eyes?

Guess my head is pretty much a bloody mess.

And how can anything be okay when I'm beginning to see things?

Yeah, Mel Morgan, astral traveler, is finally developing foresight.

Only thing is, I know for a fact it isn't as simple as a vision of the future. This thing that haunts me, that dogs my every breath, my every move, is beginning to affect my mind.

My sanity.

I stood in my frigid, steam-filled bathroom—all white ceramic tiles and dull copper—drenched in the harsh white glare of the fluorescent vanity light.

My spine remained stiff, my neck taut as I stared at the open closet door, gritting my teeth so hard they'd probably be ground smooth over time if I kept up the habit.

Though wrapped in a giant bath towel, a wave of shivers wracked my body. Tendrils of wet hair escaped a haphazard bun, and my skin was still covered in droplets of water from a super-fast shower, snaking down my neck and shoulders in icy rivulets.

My fingers curled like claws into the front of the towel, pressing it hard to my chest, some illogical part of me suddenly afraid of standing naked in the bathroom.

I took a shaky breath and narrowed my eyes, studying the inside of the closet. The shelves were filled with towels, toilet paper, detergent and other supplies, only they were an absolute, sodden mess.

Toilet cleaner and shampoo, bleach and toothpaste, mouth-wash and detergent, streaked every single towel and cloth, soaked through every toilet-paper roll, Kleenex box and cotton puff. It looked like a detergent bomb had exploded inside there.

The smell was a heady perfume of peppermint and ammonia, chlorine and lavender.

Just lovely.

Reaching out, I caught the edge of the closet door with two fingers of my free hand and swung it shut.

Then, I held my breath.

A few seconds passed and I swallowed down a bout of hyster-ical laughter as I watched the damned door swing open of its own accord.

Shifting my gaze, I avoided the fogged-up mirror because I knew what I'd see; a hazy form, just the barest shape of some-thing—of someone—reflected there, standing beside me.

Watching me.

I'm not normally a scaredy-cat. I'm the type who would

usually go in guns blazing, happy to kill demons or whoever else stood in my way of retrieving those who have been stolen.

But this evil spirit now attached to my essence, was sucking up my energy.

Someone had cursed me with this poltergeist, an evil African Black Magic spirit meant to devour my soul.

Who would do such a thing? I didn't know, but I had to find out before the curse succeeded.

I could feel it . . . slowly killing me.

Not that I could tell anyone.

Not that I *would* tell anyone.

The fisted fingers of my right hand gripped my ocher amulet as if it was a lifeline—in my case it probably was.

I forced my fingers to release their death-grip and slipped the cord over my neck. The charm—oddly shaped, the surface bumpy with the implied curves and proportions of the human form—came courtesy of Natasha, my white-witch friend.

An African ward against African magic.

She'd said it would afford me some form of protection. Maybe it wouldn't save me, but I wasn't about to decline any reprieve—however small—from the haunting of the *tokolosje*.

African black magic.

Who would have thought it possible that someone would be practicing what could be considered a dead art, and within a world already filled with an unending variety of currently-practiced magic?

I'd considered a visit to a warlock, or even handing myself over to the Supreme High Council with a plea to save my sorry ass.

Not that I would have done so, but such ridiculous thoughts had actually crossed my mind.

More than once.

Enough of a reason to believe the evil spirit was succeeding.

I inhaled sharply, stiffening my resolve. I refuse to be beaten.

More than that, I refuse to be beaten by something that didn't even have the courtesy of drawing breath.

I shut the closet door, my knuckles white as I gripped the brass handle a little harder than necessary.

As soon as it clicked closed, I spun on my heel and scurried out of the bathroom as fast as I possibly could.

My heart slammed against my ribs as I escaped the humid confines of the bathroom and shut the door behind me, the weak morning light shining in through the window, greeting me like a comforting smile.

Early morning showers—anytime showers actually—were way too dangerous these days.

I leaned against the closed door, shutting my eyes with relief. I released a very tense, very stale breath and relaxed a tiny bit. Just enough to feel a wave of frustration threaten to wash over me.

It had only been a few weeks now since I'd discovered I had an invisible, yet terrible, companion.

And I'd told only Natasha about him so far. Steph knew something odd was happening to my power, that my projections and jumps were making me weak and clumsy, but I'd held back the specifics.

And of course the Djinn Queen Aisha, who'd informed me of the spirit's existence a few weeks ago, also knew.

I'd told nobody else.

Not even Saleem.

The fewer people who knew, the better.

I knew the *tokolosje* would follow me wherever I went, but he tended to be less conspicuous when I was around other people.

I laughed to myself. My friends must be wondering what was up with me wanting to be in their company so often, especially considering I'd always preferred my privacy.

My phone buzzed and grabbing it from my nightstand, I checked the caller ID, not surprised at the unfamiliar number. I answered with a sigh, partly out of habit, partly out of responsibility.

My job required service twenty-four-seven, and a 6am call wasn't out of the ordinary.

"Mel Morgan."

"Hello? Miss Morgan?" The feminine voice was raspy, likely a garbled attempt at a husky, sexy tone.

I shook my head. *Of course it's Mel Morgan. I just answered as Mel Morgan.* "Yes?" I kept my tone neutral and polite although I was unable to stop my eyes from rolling.

The woman cleared her throat. "I'm Elise Garner. I need your help to find my son." Straight to the point. I liked that.

I found myself nodding. Maybe a case would help me get my mind off things.

"I do have some time available this week if you'd like to meet to discuss?"

After a recent last encounter with a client who'd wanted to pay for my exclusive time, I'd begun to make it abundantly clear to new clients that I always had cases going on concurrently.

"Oh?" she hesitated, "are you too busy?"

Her low tone made it sound like she was hurt that I didn't have time for her. I rolled my eyes again, wondering if I was going to be dealing with a diva. Then I straightened. It shouldn't matter, especially considering she likely had a missing family member who needed finding.

And I knew exactly how that felt.

I cleared my throat. "Not at all. I manage the cases I have as efficiently as possible and I don't take on more than two cases at a time."

"Oh. Very well. But I'm unable to meet you in person." When I didn't respond, she gave a small tinkling laugh. "I'm in Hong Kong, you see. I have a few meetings here, but even if I headed back immediately I'd only be able to meet you in two days, and I'm afraid my case is urgent."

I raised my eyebrows. "Can you tell me briefly what the case entails?"

She was silent for a long moment and just as I was about to suggest a video-conference call, she cleared her throat. "I have to speak to you in person. The . . . situation is a strange one, and what I have to tell you is quite sensitive."

With a sigh, I said, "Fine. I can arrange to meet you in the next couple hours. When are you available?"

"Oh? Are you also in Hong Kong?"

I scrambled for a response. "In transit in Taipei. I can meet in two hours if I change my flight, but only if you're certain this is urgent."

Don't waste my time. The unspoken words hung in the air.

Elise Garner laughed, the sound low and reverberating within her throat. "Don't worry, Miss Morgan. If you feel this case isn't for you, I will happily reimburse you for your flight and for your time. Is 9pm Hong Kong time good for you? The Meridian at The Garner-Royal Sun Hotel?"

That was a mouthful.

I agreed, and she rang off, but not before thanking me profusely. She left me wondering at the power held by people with money, resources and contacts at their disposal.

So many missing people would never be found because their family lacked the kind of money Elise Garner and Carlo Santiani possessed.

Still, I couldn't be negative about Santiani. He'd included me in his will—which I'd found both surprising and amazing. A letter had come with a short note which the man must have dictated to his legal team while on his deathbed.

He'd put half of his estate into a trust that issued me with a generous monthly allowance. Enough to maintain my house and provide myself, Steph and Drake with a regular income.

My only regret was that I'd received the letter *after* his death, and I hadn't been able to thank the man.

Technically, I hadn't found his daughter. Not alive, anyway.

Poor Gia Santiani had been dead a while before her father had come to me. But at least we'd managed to free her sister Gina from the demon who'd been systematically killing off Santiani's family.

Gina was still catatonic, hidden away in an up-state care facility, but the doctors had hoped she'd pull through. Just not with enough intellectual function to run her father's multinational billion-dollar business.

I still held out hope though. The impossible almost always tended to be possible in the end.

Take me for instance. I'd never have thought it possible to lie to someone I was in a relationship with.

But, here I was, lying to Saleem every single day—and with his mother's blessing no less.

We'd been gathering our resources for a mission to Mithras, the djinn plane, to look for his brother Rizwan.

Although Saleem had been resistant to me accompanying him on the mission, he'd accepted my involvement in the preparations. Probably just accepting my nosiness as proof of how much I cared. The problem was, I knew way more about his brother's situation than Saleem himself did.

Saleem—the guy I was crazy about, the guy I'd been keeping my distance from, was a djinn prince whose mother, Aisha, Queen of Mithras, Plane of the Djinn—had sworn me to secrecy with the truth of her family's precarious situation.

Back home in Mithras, Rizwan was under the control of Omega, one of the three paranormal investigative agencies within the paranormal world, and the only one accused of a whole host of nefarious, illegal and abominable activities— including abduction, wrongful incarceration, blackmail and mind control.

I could go on, because truly, the list was almost endless.

Not long ago, my shifter friend Kai Odel had discovered her

mom being experimented on by Omega. Saleem and Logan Westin—Saleem's commanding officer at Omega, and Kai's boyfriend—had begun to distance themselves from their employer ever since.

The Supreme High Council, overseer of all things paranormal across the planes, had reacted in a far more subtle way—by creating the Elite; a secret investigative agency for which they were head-hunting specific, talented mages and supernaturals.

I'd received the invitation.

And I'd been putting it off.

My excuse would be that I had way too much on my mind, but it was just that—an excuse.

CHAPTER 2

I sighed and hurried downstairs, smoothing my pants as I descended the stairs.

The black high-waisted silk pants and shimmering white blouse was a lovely, elegant combination. Completed with light make-up, freshly styled glossy black curls and gold hoops, I figured I looked professional enough for a dinner at any high-class restaurant. Even one all the way on the other side of the world.

The footwear had been a hard sell though—worlds away from my usual serviceable boots—and I'd eventually settled for six-inch-heeled knee-length boots. As was my habit, I'd tucked a dagger into each of the boots, but with heels as deadly as these, I could likely use *them* as weapons if the need arose.

Excellent thinking, Morgan.

I passed the empty kitchen and followed the glow of yellow light pooling in the hallway outside the study.

Popping my head into the room, I found Drake arranging the secret weapons-repository we'd constructed behind the closet. He turned as my heel hit a loose floorboard, and gave me a lackluster smile.

Wow. Guess I don't look that fabulous.

He must be distracted as my attire hadn't even received a raised eyebrow. "How you doing?" I watched his face, dark complexion, obsidian eyes.

Not that I really needed to ask. His glamor shivered around him in a pale haze, revealing his struggle to concentrate on keeping it up.

He didn't need to hide his real form, not while inside the house. Usually he was happy to walk around bare-faced, his blue-toned skin and black faded tattoos bare for all to see.

Today? Not so much.

Drake's mouth formed a thin line as he nodded, then returned his attention to the demon rifle—which looked familiar—that he was positioning within its slot.

"Where did you get that?"

"Your boink-buddy."

I snorted. "You know full well he isn't."

"Not yet," Drake murmured as he closed the door and walked back to the study desk. He was doing inventory, but I suspected he was performing the task just to fill time. "You two suck at romance."

"You should talk," I sank into one of the chairs bracketing the desk, "How is our favorite white witch these days?"

Drake had been helping Natasha out with the repairs to her property after a demon-witch had wrecked it. I'd begun to suspect that—despite Natasha's outward display of superior iciness—she'd kept Drake around for reasons other than physical labor.

The woman was quite capable of magically lifting a giant oak off the ground without the help of any gargoyle—no matter how cute he was.

He inhaled, long, deep and indicative of his emotional state, because Drake wasn't the type to sigh and huff. "What's up?" he asked, ignoring my question, his eyes now on the giant-sized bookkeeping spreadsheet open on the desk in front of him. Drake disliked computers and preferred to do his recordkeeping on paper. "New job?" he asked as he reached for a pen and glanced up at me.

I lifted an eyebrow. "How did you know?"

His gaze traveled pointedly from my hair to my killer heels. Then he said, "You have a certain way of speaking when you get a new case . . . a tiny hitch in your voice." His lips twitched, but he didn't smile.

I feigned shock "Wow. You scary gargoyle, you. Getting in touch with your sensitive side, I see."

He grinned, but his amusement fell short of his dark, troubled eyes, his forehead creasing as the humor dissipated.

"What's up?" I threw his question back at him.

He sighed again and put the pen down, then leaned against the backrest of the chair. "I have bad news."

"Which is?" I asked softly, already suspecting what he was about to say.

He met my gaze head on. "I'm going home for a while." I nodded. I'd been expecting this for a while now and was only surprised it had taken this long.

"When do you leave?"

"Today."

Again, no surprise. The gargoyle tended to do things on the spur of the moment.

I glanced at the ledger. "Hence the early morning stock take?"

He nodded.

"Need anything?"

He shook his head and gave me a strained smile. "You can suspend pay for the interim."

I suppressed an eye-roll. "I'll do no such thing."

He tilted his head and studied my face, his expression closed. "Why not?"

"Because you've worked just as long—and just as hard—over

the years for no pay. Just like Steph and me. Now that we can, we need to compensate ourselves for our dogged diligence toward the job."

"Dogged diligence, huh?"

I grinned. "How long will you be gone?"

He pursed his lips. "A couple weeks. I just need to speak to the family, get the lay of things."

"Will you talk to your father?"

Drake shook his head, shifting his gaze away. "I don't plan to."

He had some serious issues with Gargoyle Senior. Hopefully he'd resolve it before he got back.

"And if the opportunity comes up?"

"*If* the opportunity comes up, then I *might* talk to him. But it's not the purpose of my visit."

I sighed and got to my feet. Walking around the desk, I stopped in front of Drake and put my hands on his shoulders. "You," I gave them a squeeze and a slight shake, "take care of yourself, okay?"

He smiled and patted one of my hands absently. He was already gone, his mind on what awaited him beyond the Nexus.

I straightened, schooling my features. "I do have a case, just so you know," I sucked in a silent breath, and winced, "I'm going to Hong Kong to meet with the client."

"What?" he snapped, his tone sharp.

I shook my head. "I can do the jump. I'll make sure I take a nap before I jump back okay? And if it's too much, I'll call someone."

"The djinn?" He lifted a dark brow.

"No. Probably Bjorn." Sentinel Agent, and mutual friend of Kailin's and mine, red-headed Bjorn Larsson would provide tele-portation should I need it.

Not that I would.

"Besides, I think Saleem is being interrogated at the moment. He's out of contact and so is Logan."

"Sounds serious." Drake closed the ledger and slid it into the wide drawer in front of him.

I watched his slow, precise movements, wondering if he was still trying to stall, even on a minuscule level. "I suppose it might be serious. I'm worried Omega may try to make Saleem and Logan the fall guys. My brain is telling me they can't, because too many people know the truth," I let out a heavy sigh, "but I'm still afraid for both of them."

Drake got to his feet and stepped away, sliding the office chair neatly into place. "What did Kai have to say?"

I shook my head. "Kai's as much in the dark as I am."

She'd said as much a couple days ago when she'd rung to update me on her mom's condition. Thankfully, Celeste was much better, having regained her strength and health over the last few weeks. Kai's uncle, Niko Odel, was incarcerated, hidden away in a Sentinel facility that only his mother Ivy Odel had access to.

Which suited everyone else just fine.

Kai still harbored a deep resentment toward the man, but I hoped he'd at least receive proper psychological treatment wherever he was.

Drake's expression shifted; contemplative.

I raised a finger and waved it in his face. "Don't you even think about it, gargoyle." He looked at me, startled. I narrowed my gaze, focusing on his eyes. "I know that look. You are not changing your mind about going. I can handle the case while you're gone."

Drake grunted.

I folded my arms and rolled my eyes. "Fine. Give me a way to contact you in an emergency."

He lifted an eyebrow. "There isn't a way. Not unless I come back to check on you."

I snorted, then waved at him, shooing him off. "Then just go, already. We'll be fine. I have enough people here that I can call on. Storm, too, you know."

Mention of the Immortal seemed to satisfy Drake and he nodded, then sighed. "I have to admit I feel guilty leaving you all, but I figure it's time to do this. And get it done. Once I return, I'm never going back there again."

Drake walked to the door, and I followed. "I'd suggest you don't burn any bridges," I said softly.

His shoulders tightened. "Why should I care?" A touch of defensive with a hint of denial. Typical.

"Because you still have family there. And family is important. They define who you are. Good or bad."

"Good or bad? As in if they *are* good or bad, or if *my* definition is good or bad."

I smacked his arm. "Shut up and stop confusing me."

Drake laughed, then turned to wrap his arms around me. "I have enough family here, Mel. Even if I lose my blood family, I still have you and Steph. That's enough for me."

I submitted to the squashing, then sucked in a breath as he let me go. "Take care, my friend." I patted his cheek then watched as he turned and headed upstairs.

I didn't plan on being around for the final farewell. So like a coward, I jumped to Hong Kong.

CHAPTER 3

Ms Garner had named a prestigious restaurant—The Meridian—in downtown Hong Kong for our meeting place. The Meridian also happened to *belong* to Ms Garner.

Projecting to the guest bathroom, I checked if the coast was clear. The use of public toilets for my arrivals and departures was getting old.

The hotel restroom had just emptied of its last visitor and I teleported through, landing inside one of the cubicles on the far end.

I made one last check on the dagger in my boot. My second dagger, and a small pistol, were safely stowed inside my satchel along with a single change of clothing. I expected to have to change out of all this silk at some point.

As I left the cubicle and straightened my jacket, I ran my fingers through my hair and drew my satchel higher on my shoulder.

No need to rush in all blood-stained, looking like I'd just taken a beating.

Staring at my reflection, I ignored the shadows at the edges of my vision. The spirit seemed reluctant to show itself, which was strange. Had I managed to shake it loose?

But then I saw the blood.

It trickled down my upper lip and would have hit the stark white of my blouse had I not tipped my face over the sink in time.

Crap.

Annoyed and frustrated, I grabbed a wad of towels and wet them before scraping hard at my bloody nose. The bleeding had stopped, but I continued to rub it away, almost leaving a bruise on my upper lip.

Tears filled my eyes and I hit the marble counter with a growl of frustration. When I finally did find out who had done this to me, the bastard was going to pay.

This illness, this inability to project whenever I wanted to, was also my biggest hurdle to finding Ari.

How was I supposed to head out in search of my sister the moment I got a lead, when I had to check things out first, call Sentinel or Saleem for a lift, ensure I didn't jump too many times within a specific time period? It was slowly becoming too much to handle.

And I was getting so very tired of it.

As I stared at my reflection, I saw—in my mind's eye—Samuel's code written in the Aurora Borealis. A message he'd written for me.

I suppressed a bitter, angry laugh.

He'd probably thought I'd grab the next astral wave and come find him. Little did he know that *jumping* was soon going be the death of me.

Also, the gargoyle was going to kill me when he found out I'd lied to his face.

I wasn't getting any better and if he hadn't been so distracted with his family problems he would've seen it for himself. I had no intention of allowing Drake to blame himself though.

If I played my cards right, he'd never find out I'd lied.

I straightened, took the time to wash my face again, smooth on face cream and reapply my makeup. Then I headed out to the hotel restaurant to meet my new prospective client.

The lobby was marble everywhere, beneath my feet and on the walls, gigantic gold and crystal chandeliers hung from the three-story-high ceiling, while a huge fountain took pride of place in the middle of the floor.

I passed the splashing plumes of water, giving the dazzling display nothing more than a cursory glance as I drew to a stop at the entrance to the restaurant. I composed my features into a cool mask, waiting as the sober maitre'd approached, giving me a once-over from head to toe.

After mentioning Ms Garner's name he seemed to relax a little. He nodded then guided me to a table near the giant windows. A slim, redhead sat studying the contents of a file, her short pixie cut matching her elfin features.

Beyond her, the view of the night skyline over Hong Kong harbor was stunning, and I was pretty sure I'd never afford a table at such a prestigious place.

Oh, wait. After Santiani's generosity I probably could.

Not that I was that extravagant.

As I approached, Ms Garner looked up and I watched her expression falter. I'm not sure what she'd expected but *I* certainly wasn't what she'd hoped for.

She eyed me head-to-toe—I was getting tired of being studied this way—and I wanted to wriggle in my pantsuit, very glad now that I'd taken the time to dress a little nicer.

Whatever the woman's problem was, she covered her expression with a cool smile and nodded at the menu. "What would you like to drink?" She already had a blood-red claret at her elbow.

I returned her smiled. "A sparkling water, please," I said to the Maitre'd who gave a low bow, throwing me a genuine smile before gliding away. Perhaps the man wasn't used to kindness from the guests here if just my manners made him smile.

Elise Garner didn't wait for my drink to arrive. She leaned closer to me, her gold eyes glittering. "Are you sure you are up for this job?" She studied me as I frowned.

"I'm not entirely sure what you mean, Ms Garner."

She waved me off, airy and haughty at the same time. "You can call me Elise." She sipped her claret and set the crystal glass back on the table. "Forgive me. You just look a little too *delicate* for investigative work."

I smiled. "Not all private investigators are old, lascivious drunk males."

The waiter delivered my drink and was gone within a blink of an eye.

"Well, here's to young, lascivious drunk females then." She tipped her glass and downed her drink before setting it on the table. Then she tapped a red fingernail on the file before sliding it toward me.

I scanned the room wondering why she was so comfortable with a public display of interest in my services, but I didn't ask questions. Instead, I discretely scanned the file, and studied the photograph of the gangly teenager who looked like his worst nightmare was the discovery of one more zit.

"How long has he been gone?"

She sighed. "Two years."

I scowled. "Ms Garner . . . Elise. Can you please explain what this case is about? Was he taken? Did he run away?"

"He ran."

I sat back.

"No. Please. You don't understand. It's a little more complicated than just your average runaway."

"How do you mean?"

She sounded so sure of her words and yet what would make

her position any different from the dozens of other parents of missing children.

Maybe just her arrogance, said a little voice in my head.

"Well . . . Erik . . . he thinks he has magical abilities." She pursed her lips, her expression almost one of disgust.

I froze, ice trailing down my spine as I scanned the room a second time, hoping this wasn't some kind of trap for the hapless teleporter.

Nobody came swooping down on me, no cuffs clamped around my wrists.

"Did he leave of his own volition?"

She nodded. "He had this stupid idea that he was going to do something to save the world." She snorted, reached for her glass and made a face when she realized she'd already drained it.

"And you want me to find him and stop him?"

She nodded. "Unfortunately we can't erase the damage he's already done," she waved at the nearest waiter for another round, "but we can stop any future rash behavior on his part."

I suppressed a sigh. "What exactly is he guilty of?"

More importantly, I wanted to know why this woman was chasing after a boy who was quite likely old enough to live on his own by now. The file had said he was sixteen, and now, two years later, he'd be an adult.

She gave a short tinkling laugh that hurt my ears. "Of trying to be a freaking superhero. You have to help me stop him."

I shook my head. "A superhero? What exactly is this power?" I paused and straightened. "The power that he claims to have."

She didn't seem to notice, her eyes focused on the glass of claret being placed in front of her. "He believes he can walk through solid matter. And see through solid matter." She laughed, the sound cold, bitter and angry.

"I can see how that might pose a problem. If his powers were real." I gave her a questioning glance, sipped the fizzing water, then smiled innocently.

She laughed again, shaking her head at me. "The thing is, the stuff he's being accused of doing . . . it's looking like he does have some kind of weird ability."

"What is he doing with his power?"

Waiting in the shadows to assassinate you? I was tempted to say.

"He's stealing my money."

CHAPTER 4

*E*lise Garner had been more than generous.

She'd booked me into a suite in the very grand hotel, though she never asked if I was staying.

She just gave the maitre'd a tiny wave with her scarlet manicured fingers and he glided over with a keycard in his hand.

"You will consider the case?" she asked, handing me the file as well as a flash drive.

I nodded.

It appeared I had little choice but to nod.

Despite the fact that I felt her interest was a little too much on the monetary side.

I could decline and leave, but I preferred not to make an enemy of a woman like Elise Garner. I still had no idea how important she was, but I had already gotten the hint that she was powerful—most paranormals lived in the shadow of the human world, and often spent more time running and hiding from non-supernaturals than they did playing the stock-market and watching the daily news.

Besides, I was curious enough already to at least go over the file before I declined. So far, all I'd seen was a family falling apart and a mother failing to accept her son's differing needs.

I drained my fizzy water and got to my feet. With a smile, I grabbed the file and the keycard, and slipped the flash-drive into my jacket pocket. "I'll consider your proposal and get back to you in the morning."

"I'll meet you for breakfast in your suite. If you are still there, I'll know you'll take the case." She arched a perfectly shaped eyebrow.

With a single nod, I turned on my heel and strode out of the restaurant. The buzz of multiple conversations had begun to irritate me, resulting in a low, heavy throb at the back of my neck.

Or, that could just be my *silent partner.*

I shook my head and headed to the bank of glass boxes that posed as elevators. A uniformed bellhop waited, a tiny Asian girl with blonde hair and a toothy smile—I indulged in a bout of envy at how well she pulled the color off. I'd tried twice and had sworn never to do it again.

With white hair I just looked demonic.

The bellhop—Mai, according to her name-tag—tipped her head at me and smiled. "What floor, ma'am?"

I waved the keycard at her, revealing the number 3608. She smiled and pressed the button to open the glass doors. Inside, she stabbed the button for the top floor and my eyes widened.

Penthouse, no less.

I was officially impressed.

As the elevator rose, the silence closed in, conspicuous in the confined space. And I noticed again the absence of my evil companion, the ease with which I walked, and breathed. Knowing the only thing I had on me capable of fending it off was Natasha's African token—which I couldn't be sure even worked anymore—I scanned the glass walls of the elevator for magical wards.

Nothing but a few bright red Asian characters—probably

Chinese, but my skills were minimal when it came to Asian script —marked each corner of the doorway.

I pointed at them, giving Mai-the-bellhop a small smile, "What are those?"

She nodded slowly, and then flashed bright white teeth as she responded in an impeccable British accent. "In Chinese culture it is always good to protect one's home. Our magic men and old folk will often mark the entrances of a place of abode with signs meant to ward off evil."

I smiled, realizing too late that I probably looked too interested, or too convinced. If not both.

"So it keeps away the ghosts?" I asked, trying to appear flippant.

Mai nodded, her own expression now serious. "And evil spirits and witchcraft curses."

I pasted on a bright smile, "That's pretty cool," and was saved from further small talk when the elevator pinged our arrival.

Leaving the glass box with a small wave at my helper, I entered the hallway. My heels immediately sank into the deep pile as I headed to my door.

Judging by the number of doors leading off the long wide hallway, only eight suites occupied the top floor.

Garner was definitely using one of them, what with her name on the building itself and all. I didn't care though, even if there was a distinct possibility that she could be watching me.

For all I knew my suite was filled with cameras.

But I didn't have anything to hide. I swiped the card through the electronic reader, entered the room and paused in the hall. Because, well, there *was* a hall, a tan leather lounge suite to my left, a twelve-seater dining table to my right, and a second, less formal living area straight ahead.

Plush. Luxury. Silken. Gilded.

Nice.

I took a deep breath and dropped my satchel on the glossy

redwood dining table. Then I dialed room-service and ordered up some food.

As I rang Steph, I drew the little black mini hard-drive from my pocket and studied it.

"Hey, traveler." Steph's smile could be heard in her voice.

"Hi," I stuck a hand into the bag and rummaged around for the cable I needed, "I have a case."

"Boy, do I love those four little words."

"Not as if you don't have anything else to do." I smiled back as I connected the cable to my cell phone and attached the flash drive to the housing on the other end.

"Meh. School's boring."

"Steph. You're eighteen and your major is biomechanics. But you're a hacker. Of course, school will be boring."

She laughed. "No. It's boring 'cos the work is too easy. I could have completed the course last year."

"So? Why didn't you?"

I was acceptably stunned. Steph didn't usually talk about her smarts. The way she behaved, I'd always thought she was embarrassed by her intelligence.

"Twelve months ago, I couldn't afford to do two years' worth of papers in a single year."

"And now you can." I felt a thrill of satisfaction for Steph.

"Yes, I can. So I'll finish this year, thank goodness." I heard a loud snap and recognized Steph's signature gum-chewing habit. "Now . . . what's the deal?"

Back to business.

"Okay, I'm uploading some data from the new client's flash-drive." I could almost see Steph's evil grin. "Which I procured legitimately because she *gave* it to me." I rolled my eyes.

Steph and I had once run a small side business while I'd been still battling my teen hormonal demands. I advertised in the classifieds as a *finder of lost things* and had received random jobs.

Once, a guy had lost the keys to his Ferrari and didn't want to have new locks put in. Apparently it was the last Ferrari ever built, and he didn't want to change a thing.

So I found his keys.

And Senator Gillman's stolen coin which had apparently belonged to Abraham Lincoln.

It was only when I'd—quite by accident—retrieved the Shah of Iran's daughter Farah, saving her from her kidnappers, that I realized how much more important my cases could be.

And how much more satisfying.

Still, I continued to do high-paying jobs for mega-buck companies while finding missing people for those who couldn't afford it. Steph had said that hopefully our Robin Hood days would come to an end at some point.

Very likely *that* had just happened.

I got Steph to scan the files on the flash drive while I studied the physical file. Spreading the contents across the super-king bed in the main bedroom of the gigantic suite, I stood and stared at it.

Despite Garner's confidence, the file seemed lacking.

The cops hadn't canvassed the boy's friends well enough, hadn't tracked his whereabouts either. Garner had mentioned that the boy's vigilante activities were a secret and that she'd never, ever mentioned it to anyone.

True to her word, nothing in the file indicated the kid was up to anything illegal or nefarious.

Steph rang back ten minutes later. "So," gum cracked in my ear again, "the flash drive is pretty interesting."

"What do you have?"

"I'm sending you the info via email. Most of this shit was encrypted, as if the client wanted to ensure it would remain inaccessible if it fell into the wrong hands."

I was barely listening. My headache had gone, and I wondered again why I hadn't felt anything from the poltergeist.

Was the room warded liked the elevator?

I inspected the room, studying the threshold and window casings and found a raft of different markings.

I snapped off a few photos, determined to find out what about these symbols had worked to give me even a few minutes of reprieve from the curse.

Or if it was the symbols in the first place.

"Hey, Steph. I'm sending you a couple photographs. Can you analyze and translate them for me?"

"Sure thing, boss lady."

I snorted but didn't have time to respond as my inbox pinged new items at me every few seconds.

I scanned through them, my eyes growing ever wider.

He called himself *The Phaser* and he'd been in the news lately. He'd brought down a corrupt banking syndicate with its head office in Switzerland. He'd crushed a drug cartel in Western America by holding their money ransom.

The news had hailed him a hero. The cops had cursed him for making their security look like a joke. The people had rejoiced, and the criminals had called for him to be taken down.

I shook my head.

"Shit," I said softly.

"Yep. That's what I said too." Steph snapped her gum. "So *this* is her son?"

"According to what she said, and I'm guessing nobody would lie about something like this unless they're a little strange in the head."

"And is she?"

"Is she what?"

"Strange in the head?"

I blinked and focused. "No. A little entitled. A little preten-tious. Which is to be expected when swimming in money. Other-wise, she's just a concerned mother desperate to find her son."

"Or she's just a concerned mother desperate to stop her son from destroying her." Steph's dry tone came over the line.

"Mmh. She did mention that she wanted to stop him from stealing her money," I frowned, "Was that for real?"

"Yeah. It's interspersed with all the other cases. Attacks on banks in which Garner holds her funds. Everything from the Cayman Islands to Switzerland to South Africa. Offshore, America, it doesn't matter. He's been systematically entering and searching for something. A few times he's left with safe deposit boxes and on a number of occasions he's accessed the mainframe from inside and deleted the contents of all her bank accounts."

"Surely her insurance has paid for it."

"On a couple of occasions, he's used his own access cards to withdraw millions, negating the insurance payout."

"He has access?"

"Sole heir."

"Interesting," I pondered. "Where did her money come from?"

"She was a day-trader. Married a Texas oil baron."

"Before the oil dried up, of course."

That had been a bad move on Elise's part. But then, nobody had ever expected the oil to dry up. For centuries, oil had been mined from the depths of the earth, but anyone with two gray cells to rub together would know that mined product isn't endless, isn't self-replenishing.

Eventually, it all dried up. Like the world's oil reserves.

All gone.

Bringing cities, and countries, to a standstill.

"Someone knows her history," said Steph, sounding impressed as she cut into my thoughts. "So Elise marries Jeb Garner, gives him a son, then loses the man in a light aircraft crash when the kid is sixteen. She and the kid inherit everything, including his lucrative hotel chain, plus his string of exclusive diamond design stores. He was said to have blood diamond contacts, but nothing proven."

"Aha."

"Yeah."

"So the son hates his family wealth because he believes it's all blood money?"

"Question is . . . is it?"

"Question is . . . is it our job to care?" asked Steph lightly.

"Of course, it is. If it's blood money, then the kid is right and I'm not going to help her stop him."

"And if the kid is wrong?"

I chuckled. "Isn't it *your* job to find out, hacker?"

"Whatever," she said, deliberately snapping gum in my ear. "Right, so about your Chinese symbols."

"Yup?" I asked as a knock sounded at the door.

I opened for the food and waited as the waiter laid the meal out on a small table beside the window. He left without asking for a tip, which I supposed was a penthouse perk.

"So they are magical wards." Steph was almost blasé about it. "The symbols are ancient, dating back almost three millennia."

"But I didn't see any power attached to it."

"Apparently, they don't work like that. The Asian warlocks found a way to insert power into the written word. Process unknown."

"So these words bind a place against evil?"

"No. Everything magical," Steph paused, "Hold on. It's helping you, isn't it?"

"Yup. For the first time, I'm actually at peace."

I felt both guilty and relieved that Steph knew a little about the effects of the poltergeist, happy that she could help, and frustrated that she was on the list of suspects as one of my closest friends.

"Cool," her voice echoed on the line, "I'll recreate them for you and have them installed all around the house."

"Thanks, Steph. I'll be back in the morning."

"Your morning?"

Time zones were annoying, even in the normal world. When jumping to different planes, keeping track of the drastic changes in time was a bitch, and so much worse than earth time zone issues.

"Yeah, Hong Kong time. I have until the morning to decide if I'm taking the case." I recalled the look Garner had given me. Something between desperation and demand.

Which put me somewhere between willing and unwilling to help her.

"So . . . are you taking the case?"

"What do you think?"

I knew why Steph wanted me to take it. Not to help Garner, but to save her son from getting caught.

Unfortunately for Garner, Steph and I were of the same mind.

CHAPTER 5

$\mathcal{I}$n the peaceful privacy of the hotel suite I did all the things I would have done at home.

I soaked in the tub.

Only the bath was twice the size of mine, and almost as deep as a hot tub, *and* it was filled with scented water, sparkling dust and rose petals.

The best part of it? The water didn't try to drown me, I didn't slip or fall, and nothing broke. Not even a single crystal glass or perfume decanter or shampoo bottle.

I ate a delicious dinner.

Only the meal—kobo beef and Szechuan noodles—was cooked by a five-star culinary wizard with things like Michelins on his belt. A single meal would probably cost more than I made on a single case.

I drank an awesome red wine.

A ridiculously exclusive cab sav from the Napa Valley's last batch known to man. Drake's contact would have been cheaper.

But the best, and most important, part of my evening? The fact that I had experienced all of these normal, mundane things in total, absolute peace.

Without the burden of the evil spirit. Without a care about nosebleeds, and headaches and cupboards opening without anything touching them.

Here in the hotel room in Hong Kong, I was safe from the poltergeist that haunted me.

And I was most reluctant to leave its safe confines.

But I had to.

~

I'd dressed in a pair of black satin pajamas—a birthday gift from Drake because apparently he didn't believe that sleeping in my underwear was an acceptable thing—and had just checked the messages on my cell phone when the door slammed open and two men rushed in.

Taken by surprise, I failed to teleport fast enough, and ended up with my mouth taped, a black hood over my head and silver cuffs around my wrists.

I had managed to drop my cell phone into my pajama pocket, though. One possible avenue to freedom.

I'd been taken so fast that both the daggers in my boots were probably laughing at me right now.

So much for being able to take care of myself.

Disgusted, more with myself than anything, I jabbed my elbow into ribs and guts and whatever other body parts I could reach, frustrated by the darkness that hampered my vision.

Although I elicited a few groans and a couple of lines of profanity that I couldn't understand, my two captors never let go.

Whoever these men were, they knew I had abilities beyond that of a normal human being. Hence the silver cuffs.

The two thugs manhandled me, each gripping an upper arm as they tried to push me toward the doorway. I had two choices. Struggle and give them hell, or play it cool and get as much info as I could.

Then, hope like hell I find a moment alone to use my weapons or teleport the heck out of this mess.

I relaxed and let them lead me out of the hotel suite—so much for five-star security—and toward the elevators. Heading straight past and on toward the door to the stairwell, they took me one flight up.

The door opened on a gust of muggy late-night air.

The low throb of the rotating blades of a helicopter reverberated through my bones, thrusting air at me in unrelenting blasts.

The two thugs bundled me inside the chopper and the small craft took flight, zipping through the Hong Kong night, destination unknown.

Only a few minutes, probably no more than three, had passed when the chopper banked to the right and hovered as the pilot confirmed his intention to land.

He touched down smoothly, and I was annoyed at being impressed with his technical skill while in the process of being abducted, and he being party to said abduction.

The thugs hustled me out of the chopper, one tossing me over his shoulder like a sack of potatoes.

Probably wise, as I'd begun to lose my patience with them and had delivered a swift hard double-footed kick to one of them, connecting with the family jewels.

We entered a second stairwell, the density of the air around me changing with the thudding of boot-heels and metallic clatter of skin against metal banisters.

They halted after two flights, then paused as a door whooshed open for them. Despite being blind to my surroundings, it was easy to keep track of my location.

They certainly weren't doing a good job of subterfuge.

They marched along a corridor, this one with carpets just as plush and deep as at Garner's hotel. Another short halt as a card was swiped and a second door glided open.

Inside the room, the change in temperature proclaimed that the owner preferred things slightly cooler than most.

My transport slid me off his shoulder to my feet, then sat me down backward. I dropped inelegantly into a chair and heard my satchel thud onto the floor beside me.

At least they'd had the sense to bring my stuff with me.

Very thorough.

I caught the scent of incense in the air and sat back, figuring it was much better to remain calm. There was absolutely nothing I could do right now. The metal cuffs hummed against my skin and I could feel the magic teasing my bones.

Despite my taped mouth, I wanted to tug at my cuffs, and scream at my captors.

I had shit to do.

I didn't have time for abductions and illegal incarcerations.

I didn't have time to be stupid and careless either and I'd done just that. Drake was going to be so pissed off. He'd spend not a single moment in sympathy for my plight. I could just hear him snort and say I'd asked for it because I was so fucking complacent.

He'd be right.

I wiggled my bare feet. Bound too, but the bite of plastic said 'zip ties'.

I tested the tape with my tongue, wetting it with saliva over and over and moving it back away from my lips as far as I could get it. Still, I felt helpless especially with the black hood blocking out all signs of light.

Nothing moved in the apartment for a while, until finally a door opened in the distance. They must have left me in an interior room.

This high up, I'd likely be in a private apartment but I wasn't planning on getting too comfortable.

At least I didn't have to pee.

Yet.

I was nodding off, after what felt like hours, when I heard someone yelling.

My head snapped back as the sound of a harsh voice drew closer. Close enough to clarify that he wasn't yelling but rather speaking very loudly in Chinese. He sounded angry, annoyed and very short-tempered.

The door slammed open and the speaker hurried toward me and whipped off the hood. Bright light assaulted my eyes, making everything dark and hard to define.

More Chinese now, this time louder yelling.

I watched the larger thug, his face twisted with worry as he carefully peeled off the tape covering my mouth.

The speaker came around to stand in front of me, and I tried to contain my surprise.

I'd heard of Kitsune, but having never seen one I had to admit I was enthralled. The man was elegant, tall, well-built, his pointed nose and hollow cheekbones making him look very . . . foxy.

And he wore a salmon-pink tailored suit.

The only thing setting him apart from any normal human was the fox-tail that swung from the base of his spine.

Though well-glamored from human eyes, it wasn't hidden from me.

I stared at the tail, then back up at the man's knowing eyes.

"You know what I am?" A canine caught the light and glinted as he smiled.

I nodded. What was the point in lying?

"Do you know *who* I am?" he asked, leaning forward to undo the zip ties.

I braced myself for the jump when the cool blade of a knife grazed my ankles. "I do hope you will forgive my useless staff."

The man leaned closer, sawing the zip ties, then smiled as they gave a small snap. I steeled against the urge to back away from his teeth—I dealt with shifters all the time but this one set me on edge. Maybe it was the whole abduction thing that made me wary.

Only the twinkle in his eye made me wonder if he was just playing with me.

"So? *Who* are you?" I lifted a brow as he tucked the plastic ties into his jacket pocket and stood.

He scowled, then straightened, tugging at the lapels of his jacket. "My name is Jon Tanaka."

I nodded, my bare feet having made me aware that I'd been caught unarmed as well, my daggers and gun all still inside my hotel room. "Hello, Jon Tanaka. I'd like to say that it's a pleasure to meet you, but I also pride myself on being honest."

He grinned. "Ah. A sense of humor," the kitsune began to pace in front of me, "I apologize if you were frightened. You were not meant to be harmed in any way, physically or emotionally. My employer would be very unhappy if you were unhappy."

"I feel sorry for your employer, because I *am* unhappy," I glared at him.

He grinned again and I was beginning to tire of his cheerful smile.

Then Tanaka inhaled sharply, as if remembering something, then met my gaze head on. "My employer will be along shortly." He bowed low. "Again, I apologize for any discomfort. My men will ensure you have something to eat in the interim."

Then he left in a flurry of orange dust. I raised an eyebrow at the empty spot. Then glance around me. One of the guards, the smaller one this time, stood beside the door, arms folded, shades hiding his eyes.

I gave him a thin smile then got to my feet and massaged my wrists. Walking over to the window, I stared out at the Hong Kong skyline. The building was across the city from the Garner hotel.

Did Garner know what had happened to me?

Or perhaps *she* was the one who'd set me up. Was her son real, or were all those articles just a fiction created using internet search engines?

I shook my head and folded my arms, feeling the bulge of my cellphone in the pocket of my pajama shirt.

Facing the window, I retrieved the phone, set it on silent and sent a message to Steph telling her where I was and what had happened. She replied within seconds saying she was already tapping into the hotel's security feed.

Then I shut the phone and glanced over my shoulder.

"I thought there was food," I asked with a thin smile.

He gave a short nod, opened the door, spoke a few words to someone outside and then returned to his original position.

Great. That meant he wasn't leaving anytime soon.

I should be grateful they'd removed the zip ties. I still wore the cuffs though, which prevented me from teleporting right out of there.

A few minutes later, a tray arrived with coffee, a fruit salad, yogurt and toast—breakfast in the middle of the night. How nice.

I sat at the table and ate quickly, drinking the dark coffee while watching both the guard in the reflection of the window, and the view beyond it. The sky remained a murky black, thick clouds of pollution marring the city skyline.

The long length of metal chain that attached each of the silver cuffs, allowed me to move comfortably and I began to accept that I wasn't here as a captive.

Not technically, anyway.

Or was I just lying to myself? I was, after all, not allowed to leave.

The door glided open so slowly that I didn't even notice until the shape of a man moved on the threshold. I rose to my feet, watching Tanaka enter, his expression broadcasting that something big was about to happen.

He turned on his heel and looked at someone beyond my line

of sight, bowed repeatedly and walked backward as his boss entered the room.

Nothing changed around me and yet everything changed.

The air felt lighter, against my cheek, and in my lungs as I inhaled.

A man entered, form and features swathed within a white hooded cloak. The stranger was thin and tall, even taller than his fox lackey. From the shadowed depths of his cowl, his eyes glittered silver.

Then he stepped closer and I blinked hard.

He watched me with an unnatural yet non-intrusive intensity, his face a pale alabaster. Long silver hair flowed from beneath the hood and I gave a short nod as it hit me.

I was looking at an Immortal Ancient.

CHAPTER 6

Within the supernatural world, the Ancients were designated as Immortals. Made up of Titans, Ancients, Angel and Gods, as well as human-origin immortals, the Immortals were the most long-lived and the most glorified of beings.

Of the four main categories, the Ancients were named so because they were the oldest of beings, rumored to be even older than the gods. Where gods rose and fell, the ancients were ever existent.

Ancients were hardly ever known to reveal themselves to mortals.

And if they did, nobody talked about it.

So, the fact that I was shocked into silence was completely understandable. But this particular ancient took my silence the wrong way.

The ancient tilted his head, his hood slipping from his brow, then falling to his shoulders to reveal aquiline features, and intense silver eyes which pierced the kitsune.

"Jon? What happened?" His voice, though soft, held a strong

note of disappointment, lashing out at Tanaka with such intensity that he flinched.

"I'm sorry, my Lord, I didn't mean for her to be hurt," Tanaka said, his face turning red. I almost felt sorry for him. He hesitated, then glanced at me for a moment before focusing on the ancient again. "The boys got a little rough with her while they were retrieving her. I did tell them not to hurt her."

My chin rose an inch. "I don't particularly fancy being abducted," I said pointedly, watching the neutrality of the ancient's expression.

His composure made me wonder if Elise Garner had something to do with this.

The ancient's silver gaze shifted to my face, and he tipped his head, his expression far away as he considered my words.

Draped in a calm, stillness, he exuded peace, as if silence was his way, and speech was not required unless completely necessary.

Then he took a breath and stepped toward the kitsune. Tanaka's lips quivered as words I didn't understand fell from his lips— a whispered mantra of apologies. He lowered his head, baring his neck as if offering it on a chopping block.

Woah.

I cleared my throat. "I'm fine, though. They didn't hurt me."

Both ancient and kitsune glanced sharply at me. But neither was as surprised as *I* myself was at coming to Tanaka's defense— too late to take it back now. When he snapped a grateful glance at me, his lips curving again into his annoyingly cheerful smile, I let out a tense breath.

The ancient straightened, folded his long pale fingers in front of his waist and watched my face, contemplative, and serene again. "You do not need to defend him, Melisande. He must take responsibility for his own actions."

"I understand. But I didn't give them much choice. I fought

them pretty hard. Maybe . . . if I'd come quietly . . . they would not have needed to subdue me?"

I was thinking about my foot, and the solid contact it had made with the man's family jewels and almost winced at the memory of his high-pitched squeal.

The ancient took a step closer and the air around me hummed, electric energy enveloping me. "You would defend these men?" He didn't hide the curiosity in his voice.

I swallowed hard. "If you are going to hurt them, then yes. I so don't need anyone hurt in my name. I don't think I could live with the Karma."

The ancient smiled—likely his version of bursting into laughter at my stunning wit—and beckoned me toward the dining table beside the floor-to-ceiling window. My answer must have satisfied him, considering the lack of maiming inflicted on the kitsune.

Oddly enough, I found myself so very relieved.

"Come, Melisande. We need to speak. We have wasted enough time already."

I obeyed, figuring I couldn't refuse an *ancient*, and I was far too curious not to play along. I slid into the chair and laid my cuffed wrists on the table in front of me.

The ancient's silvery eyebrows curved, and he looked over at Tanaka, his eyes darkening in disappointment.

"I'm sorry, my Lord. We couldn't be sure she wouldn't just teleport away if we didn't bind her."

Tanaka bowed and scurried forward, pulling keys from his pocket and rattling the chain far harder than was necessary. The cuffs clicked open, and I felt a rush of magic against my skin, as if a ward had just been lifted away. Tanaka straightened and pocketed the cuffs, I rubbed the tender skin at my wrists.

I sent him a dark glare. "All you had to do was ask me."

Tanaka met my eyes, his cheerful smile toned down somewhat. "If I had told you that an ancient wished your attendance, would you really have listened and come with me?"

Pausing, I opened my mouth to respond, then discovered I didn't have an appropriate answer. I clamped my jaw shut, trying hard not to smile. "Point taken."

The room was silent now, so quiet that I could hear the air entering and leaving my nostrils.

Long moments later, the ancient said, "I do apologize for the subterfuge in obtaining your attention." I shrugged. "My name is Darius. And I need your help."

I sucked in a shocked breath as slowly as I could, positive now that I was dreaming.

Darius smiled. "I know it's a little hard to absorb, but I tracked you down a few days ago and have made every attempt to gain access to you, but something was blocking me."

I frowned. "My wards?"

He shook his head. "Your white witch is powerful, but she can't keep an ancient out."

Pasting on a polite smile, I found I felt a lot less comfortable knowing the ancients could come and go as they pleased—even into my home. And I couldn't stop them.

Ignoring his all-knowing words, I asked, "How may I help you?"

He offered a short nod, "We've been looking for someone . . . for a long time. Centuries, if I were to be honest. And I believe we have finally found her."

"Me?" My heart slammed against my ribs, a strange amalgamation of fear and worry surging up into my throat, a drowning sensation I didn't much enjoy.

The corners of his mouth lifted in a soft smile. "No, my dear. The one we seek is of great danger to the existence of all the planes."

What did *I* have to do with it? I wanted to ask, but my gut said that impatience wouldn't go down well with Darius.

He got to his feet and began to pace, long sweeps back and forth in front of the glass window, the fabric of his pure white cloak swishing around his knees.

The darkness beyond turned the glass into a mirror and I watched his face as he stopped and turned to stare out at the Hong Kong night.

His silver eyes, shining from the depths of his shadowed sockets, gave him a corpse-like appearance.

How old was Darius, the Ancient?

His voice broke through my thoughts. "Centuries ago a child was born, a child so filled with darkness that everyone, even the Immortals were afraid. They set a curse upon the soul, binding it so that it would die within years of its birth.

"We lost track of this Black Soul until a few weeks ago. It began as blips on our radar. Our sorcerers are excellent trackers and they sensed the energy of the Dark One. I tracked it to Reykjavik a few weeks ago."

He stopped and watched my shocked gaze in the window's reflection. "Samuel?" I asked softly. It simply isn't possible. Samuel was my mentor and he had a heart of gold.

"No," Darius sighed and turned to face me, "but when he opened the way to access your mind, he allowed our trackers to see through the gap in the curtain of the Veil. The Dark one lives there, where Samuel is. If we could only access it through him we would, but we are well aware of his . . . health situation."

More than just a situation.

"It could kill him. He's barely holding on as it is," I leaned forward on my seat, "What can I do to help you?"

"Not a single thing until we solve *your* predicament."

Confusion clouded my mind. What was he talking about?

He chuckled. "You are feeling well today, are you not?"

Oh, that.

I nodded stiffly, rubbing the spot on my wrist that had been chafed by my silver jewelry. "Yeah. Since I arrived in Hong Kong.

I suspect it's those wards I'm seeing everywhere I go. Is it Chinese magic?"

As I spoke I scanned the room, nodding at the red symbols painted onto the walls on either side of the entrance to the room.

Darius shook his head. "It's ancient magic. A ward against the evil dead."

I let out a huff. "So it's still with me?"

He gave a sad smile. "Unfortunately, yes. The ward keeps it blocked. Almost as if it's asleep. While you are within the wards, it won't trouble you as much."

"Like a magical sedative?" I rubbed my forehead automatically, then paused. I didn't have a headache. Not one caused by the *tokolosje* anyway. "What do I do to get rid of it?"

"You need to find the one who put the spell on you."

I sighed and sat back. "Needle in a haystack." I stared out at the skyline. "I've wracked my brain trying to figure out who it could be." My voice was soft, almost as if I was speaking to myself, but I knew he'd heard me.

"Perhaps the perpetrator is closer than you think." His suggestion had my head snapping up so fast, the bones in my neck gave a loud crack.

"You're saying one of my friends did this to me?" My head grew hot and my ears began to ring.

Darius raised a hand. "Hush, child. Remain calm." After I took a few deep breaths, he returned to his seat. "What I am saying is . . . it could be a stranger, an enemy, or a friend. But finding the spellcaster is the key."

"This is African magic," I shook my head, "I don't even know anyone who performs such spells."

"*You* don't have to know someone."

Defeated, I sighed and sat back. "So what happens when I find this person?"

"Then we use his, or her, life to break the spell."

I stared aghast at the Ancient. "You mean we have to kill the one responsible?"

Darius didn't answer. He just watched me as my brain turned the whole problem over, looking for the solution.

At last, I snapped my fingers. "We need their blood." A short nod.

"Which means we need to find them first, and contain them long enough to obtain some blood."

Another nod.

"Is blood the only thing that will work?" He squinted at me. "What other biological samples could we use?" I asked.

It only made sense since I tracked people using anything containing DNA, or even a micro sample of blood.

I tracked their essence, found in abundance within living tissue, blood, hair, nails, and even bone marrow. Although, I usually steered clear of the last option.

He sat forward, elbows on the table now. "This is true. I do believe that any living part of the spellcaster will be sufficient to help break the curse."

I got to my feet. It was my turn to pace.

Then I stopped as an idea hit me. "You have a plan?" asked Darius with a gentle smile.

Do ancients read minds?

I struggled to recall, but then put it aside and focused, "If I can discreetly obtain biological samples from each of the people I come in contact with on a regular basis, we can use that to rule them out one at a time?"

Darius was already nodding, looking at me the way a proud parent would a child prodigy.

"I like your plan. Discrete. It will not destroy your relationships, and will allow you to eliminate the innocent without alerting the guilty party to your distrust."

I snorted. "When you put it that way, it doesn't sound like the best of plans anymore."

Folding my arms, I stared at him. I was suffocating beneath an avalanche of crazy. What the hell was happening to my life, anyway?

One moment I had a handful of regular problems, social or emotional shit, to deal with. Now there's a Dark One—who sounded like deep trouble—and the impending total destruction of the world—even deeper trouble—on the line.

And now I had to sneak around and steal blood and hair from my friends and loved ones, just so I could rule them out as the traitor who wants me dead.

You just couldn't make this shit up.

CHAPTER 7

Tanaka had delivered me back to my hotel with profuse apologies, his cheerful smile distinctly absent.

He left me with his and Darius's email addresses and cell numbers, as well as a drop location for the DNA samples I was meant to begin collecting as soon as I got home.

The kitsune had promised to also provide me with anything I needed; information, arms, backup and more.

He'd left in a hurry, still subdued in the wake of Darius's disapproval. Tanaka, with his departure, seemed to have taken my energy with him.

Perhaps it was my adrenaline crashing, but I could do nothing other than crawl beneath the covers, my limbs telling me in no uncertain terms that I was done.

I lay in the bed, spent from the unexpected activities of the night, fatigue pulling at my muscles, forcing myself to stay awake just a few minutes longer.

I had one more thing to do, and considering I had the time forced onto me by Elise's expectation of a morning meeting to confirm my interest, I planned to use it.

Honestly, I'd have preferred to go straight home, but as interested as I was in the case, I didn't want to jeopardize it especially since the woman seemed to already have misgivings with reference to my physical appearance.

Still, the time did allow me the opportunity for a quick projection.

Darius's mention of Reykjavik had fueled my need to revisit the scene. Slipping into the Ether, I began my search, tracing my way back to the Northern Lights where Samuel had led me not so long ago.

I floated there, sensing the air around me, sending out my consciousness, hoping for even the slightest hint of Samuel's feedback.

My senses spread out like a radar, testing the waves of energy within the ether. A few minutes later—and just when I was beginning to tire—I bumped into a thin, fading trail of Samuel's essence.

The ether occupied a space between the worlds, and unlike on Earth, gravity didn't exist there. Everything within the ether simply remained where it was, unless encouraged to do otherwise.

Or unless time broke it down into minute particles that end up absorbed back into the ether itself.

The feedback existed, connected between places, connected between worlds, because its energy gives it impetus.

Energy of its owner.

Time ages everything including feedback, so I was supremely lucky to have found Samuel's.

I grasped onto his threads and followed it carefully.

Slowly.

I usually tracked feedback at lightning speed, confident of my ability to navigate the ether, confident that I wouldn't lose hold of a thread.

But, perhaps because it was Samuel—or because it somehow connected me with Ari—I took the greatest care with tracking him.

The energy pulled me along, my heart going ever faster, until it stopped mid-air.

There one moment.

Gone the next.

I hovered for a few seconds, stunned. Where had it gone?

Feedback threads fade away. I knew that. But they don't just cut off as if an invisible wall had slammed down on it.

Continuing along, I followed in the direction the feedback had originally been heading, but too soon I became lost in a highway of feedback traffic.

I slowed to a stop, staring at the streams of colors around me, hopelessness washing over me.

It wasn't easy to pick up a broken thread in the first place, and near impossible in the tangled mess of energy lines I now faced.

Stunned, disappointed and exhausted, I returned to my body, wondering what Darius would say should I tell him of my failure. Worse, what would Samuel and Ari think when they found out I'd failed to find them, that I could track strangers for a living, but not the people I loved the most.

Tears trailed down my face and I turned over and hugged my pillow. I needed rest after what I'd been through during the day, and more so after what the *tokolosje* had put me through in the past few weeks.

The hauntings, merely annoying at first, were steadily getting worse.

Hopefully, I'd be able to stop him before he killed me.

~

J cracked open my eyes, wincing against the pale light streaming into the hotel room window. Weak as it was, it still managed to sear its way into my brain and I turned over with a groan, pulling the pillow over my head.

I'd fallen asleep hard after the projection. Not surprising considering the constant fatigue I experienced. More so since the wards had given me a small respite from the rigors of my haunting.

Still, I'd barely gotten sleep enough to qualify as rest. I had a list of things to do and far too little time in which to do it.

When the doorbell went half an hour later, I'd changed into fresh clothes, still as elegant and still as businesslike, boots on, firearm and daggers stowed, and satchel ready.

The white silk pants and sapphire blue peasant blouse wouldn't appeal to Garner—not that I gave a damn about her preconceived notion of what an investigator ought to look like.

I'd bought the pants and blouse a year ago for Governor Kruik's ball—where I'd posed as a reporter in order to arrest the man for trading in paranormal slaves—and hadn't worn them since.

I'd thrown them into my satchel only because they were thin and hadn't needed ironing, and they folded up really small so I didn't need to lug around an extra bag.

Taking a moment, I projected quickly, the tracker version of a peephole, and confirmed my visitor was in fact Elise Garner.

Dragging stiff fingers through my hair, I headed to the door and opened it for her, still annoyed that I'd had to stick around for this confirmation meeting.

She stood on the threshold, spine stiff, tension and worry etching her face in a network of fine lines. The woman's face suggested her age at more than a decade older than her fifty.

"So . . . you'll take the case." Her face revealed not a sign of emotion, although I hadn't missed that slight hesitation in her voice.

"I will. But I can't stay for breakfast. I have to return to Taipei. I can no longer ignore my current case." I'd almost forgotten about the Taipei lie.

I received a curt nod. "I expect daily updates."

"I'll send you an email. Or my partner will, if I'm unable."

She nodded again, scanning me from head-to-toe. When she met my eyes she said, "I suggest you start carrying a weapon. Or learn some martial arts. A girl like you can disappear very fast if she can't defend herself well."

"A girl like me?" I didn't explain that I had already ticked those two boxes courtesy of the gargoyle and Storm.

I didn't say that right at that moment I had two very sharp, very dangerous Persian daggers tucked inside each of my boots.

Nor did I tell her I had a metal-fae pistol in my satchel, filled with bullets that could kill a demon, its trigger just waiting to be pulled.

She lifted an eyebrow. "My dear, the last thing a woman who looks like you should be doing is detective work. It's dangerous. It's not my place to question your motives, but even *I* had to go out on a limb to trust you."

I smiled. "I assure you, Ms Garner, I've never had a complaint in the past. And in fact, this is the first time my appearance has come under a client's scrutiny."

And this is the last time I'm ever going to wear silk to a first meet.

Garner left soon after, taking my bank details with her and promising to make a swift deposit. She'd been generous, but these days I concentrated more on the job than on the money.

Amazing how priorities changed when you had access to regular funds. The thought of those funds reminded me that I needed to check on Gina. Which in turn reminded me that I needed to check on Samuel.

And Saleem

And the Murdochs.

As I packed my bag and prepared to leave, I considered having a dinner party at my place and inviting all the non-catatonic people on my list. That would tick off the majority of the boxes in one go.

The catatonic contingent, I'd have to go see in person.

CHAPTER 8

*H*ome at last.

Felt so good.

After a hot shower—intended to relax my stiff muscles after the jump—and a change into yoga pants and an extra-large tee, I checked my pistol and then my dagger, more out of habit than necessity.

I'd lost the soap six times even though I'd stowed it safely on the shower shelf. I'd ended up scalding myself when the cold water stopped flowing so suddenly I hadn't had time to get out of the stream. I'd slipped on the wet floor and landed on my hip after the bath mat had mysteriously moved to the other side of the bathroom.

Honey, I'm home.

Thank goodness I'd decided I was too tired to shave my legs. That may not have ended well.

I'd been super careful with my toothbrush, a little reluctant to die considering the very high likelihood of impaling myself in the throat, or poking an eye out. In the end, I'd escaped the dangers of the bathroom with clean teeth, a sore ass and very red burn on my shoulder.

The bathroom wasn't the only dangerous place in the house for me, though it felt like the *most* deadly to me.

I was going to have to do something about this pest soon.

Like yesterday.

I sat heavily on the bed and sent a text to Darius asking him for more details about the wards. A few minutes later he responded to say he'd emailed me a scanned copy of the wards and instructed me to find a kitsune sorcerer.

Apparently fox shifters were known to have a specific power which allowed them to generate such wards with ease. Only problem was, sorcerers were few and far between, and finding one who was also a kitsune would not be as simple as browsing the online phonebook.

Next, I sent a text to Natasha—the best person to track down a sorcerer of any kind.

Message sent, I lay back down and closed my eyes.

Before I could even pray for sleep, I sank deep into unconsciousness.

~

*A*rriving in the kitchen a few hours later, the sound of someone pacing the floor of my living room spiked my curiosity level to the max. The stove was empty, no bubbling pots, despite the dinner hour.

Yes.

No gargoyle chef.

My heart tightened. I missed him already.

Gathering that if my living room pacer was inside the ward, then someone had let him in and he wasn't here to assassinate me. Not with that brand of serious pacing.

Most likely Saleem.

The thought of him sent a little blast of warmth to my heart.

I stepped toward the hall, but halted as a chorus of soft creaks echoed around the kitchen.

Swallowing the urge to both groan and shriek with anger, I did a slow 360 to find every single cupboard door hanging open.

Not surprised.

Creeped out. But not surprised.

I debated whether to leave the doors that way, but eventually gave in and began to close them from one side of the kitchen.

As I made a full circuit of the room, angrily closing my mom's old cupboard doors, I held in the urge to scream at the evil spirit.

The fucking poltergeist was back, and with a vengeance.

I rushed around the cupboards, shutting doors—holding back the need to slam them hard—only to arrive right back where I'd started with all those doors open again. I let out a frustrated sob and began to close them faster, my frustration fueling my movements.

Again, after I'd completed a full circuit of maniacal door-shutting, I reached the threshold only to discover that they were all open again. Tears slipped down my cheeks and my fingers curling into fists at my side

I must have slammed a door or two a little harder than intended, because someone cleared their throat behind me.

I stiffened.

"What the fuck is going on here?" asked Saleem, his husky voice unusually lost on my libido.

I turned slowly and met his concerned eyes, aware that my own were wet and probably unflattering.

All the cupboards were wide open again and it had to look pretty strange to any observer.

I shrugged and smiled. "I'm just doing a bit of cleaning," I said my voice deceptively innocent.

"Cleaning, huh?" he folded his tattooed arms and leaned against the doorjamb, a cool smile curving his luscious mouth, his jet-black curls sweeping against his shoulders.

His expression said I was full of shit.

"Yeah," I mumbled as I began to shut the doors. "I was looking for something and then I ended up moving stuff and eventually I figured why not? I might as well set them because certainly nobody else keeps anything in order h—"

"You're babbling."

"And a girl is not allowed to babble?" I didn't look back at him.

"Not when she's frustrated and crying."

I stopped at the opposite end of the kitchen, dropping my fingers to the edge of the stove. Sniffing, I wiped my face with the back of my hand.

"That time of the month," I muttered.

Saleem gave a snort-laugh. "You'd be the first woman I know that has ever been haunted by a poltergeist at that time of the month. Talk about PMS."

I spun on my heel and glared at him, somewhere between relieved and scared. "I'm not haunted. Don't be silly."

A little too high with the pitch of the voice there, Mel.

Saleem lifted an eyebrow and pointed at my face.

I frowned. What he was on about?

"Your nose is bleeding."

"Shit." I grunted, held my hand over my nose and eyed the box of Kleenex on the counter near his elbow. He turned, grabbed a stack and hurried over to me. He handed it over with an unamused grin, then leaned against the edge of the kitchen table.

Giving him a murderous glare, I snatched the tissues from his hand and cleaned up my dripping nose.

Then I offered the ruby-red stain on the tissue, a hateful glare all of its own. I would not be surprised if I were to find the stain contained a significant percentage of my much-needed brain cells.

Rolling my eyes, I tossed the Kleenex into the trashcan and met Saleem's gaze. He'd sat there all this while without saying a word, with that disappointed-slash-worried expression on his face, patiently waiting for me to talk.

I placed my hands on my hips, and lifted chin defiantly. "What?"

"I've been wondering what was up with you. Strange silences, avoidance behavior, increased incidence of nosebleeds, constantly looking over your shoulder, edgy, snappy—"

"Okay, okay. Fine, Mr Tracker-whisperer." I headed to the table and sat slowly, giving Saleem a pointed look.

He took the hint and moved slowly to the seat opposite me. He looked calm, but the black tattoos on his forearms swirled across his skin, glamor fading with his magical concentration.

I rested my elbows on the table and placed my chin on my palms. "I'm so fucked."

Saleem snorted and leaned closer. "Care to elaborate a little?"

"What the hell," I looked up with a pained sigh, "I'm cursed."

Saleem nodded, made a rolling motion with his hand. "A little more *elaborate* than that."

I rested my forehead on my hands and gripped my head tightly, letting out a low groan. "Someone—apparently a dude with a sick sense of humor, and a black hole for a heart—has put a curse on me. So, now I have an evil spirit along for a ride everywhere I go. And not only is he in my constant company, he also makes my nose bleed, drains my energy and oh wait—this is the best part—he's a freaking psycho poltergeist who opens doors, drops soap on tiles so I slip and fall, and may even think it's funny to turn on the garbage disposal for kicks so don't go dropping anything in-"

"Mel," Saleem's voice was loud, and in front of my face as he shook me by the shoulders, hard, "Mel."

I blinked, staring straight into his face. I was on my feet, my limbs taut, my spine stiff with frustration.

Saleem's face went from tight and gray, to a more healthy looking relaxed. "That's good. At least I didn't have to slap you."

"Yeah, buddy. Physical abuse would not bode well for you. Ugh," I held my head, "what happened?'

He shrugged, then sat on the table. "You were talking. Then you were ranting. Then you got to your feet and started getting a little too hysterical for my liking."

"Oohh, don't like hysterical females, do we?" I snapped, wondering why I was so touchy all of a sudden.

"I don't mind hysterical females at all. Just the ones about to stab me through the eye with a dagger. *Those* ones tend to put me a little on edge."

"Huh?" I followed Saleem's chin-jerk to my dagger which now lay on the table, instead of in my boot. "What the hell is going on?" I whispered, my legs suddenly unable to support my weight.

As I sank to the floor, I felt arms go around me, holding me gently. "I know," Saleem chuckled, "I have this effect on woman all the time."

With dramatic flair, he scooped me up in his arms and waggled his eyebrows.

"What?" I frowned. "You knock women unconscious?"

He clicked his tongue and I hid my smile as he carried me to the living room. "No. They swoon because they can't handle how hot I am."

He laid me down on the long sofa and tucked a cushion under my head and I gave a soft snort. "Mmh. Good luck with that. Guess you spend too much time reviving your weak women to leave time for anything else."

My head spun, my muscles still tight and tense, and yet I was still able to feel a rush of fury at the thought of Saleem with *other* women.

Saleem, grinning way too widely for my liking, sat beside me on the sofa. "At least I know I have the best ability of all."

"Which is?"

"Being able to get a woman flat on her back without her even realizing it." His eyes twinkled and I would have sat up and kissed the freaking life out of him if the room hadn't been spinning so crazily.

I just lay there, staring at the ceiling, frustrated.

Pissed off.

Pissed off was good.

Shifting my gaze to Saleem's face, I asked, "By the way . . . what are you doing here?" He put his hand on his heart, his expression fake-hurt. "Aren't you supposed to be all up in Omega's grill 'cos of Celeste?"

Saleem nodded. "Logan's got that covered. Seems like the bigwigs aren't really interested in us."

"Because you're clean?" I struggled into a sitting position. Saleem sat beside me, resting my legs on his lap.

He shook his head. "That and more, but we have yet to understand it. Something is fishy with Jess too, but she won't say what, and Storm's been acting so strange these past few days . . ."

"Strange how?"

"Strange like he knows something we don't. He's been a little too short-tempered as well."

I lifted an eyebrow. "Not with me. He's probably just preoccupied. A lot of crazy shit's been happening."

Which was true. Storm tended to take on the burden of anyone and everyone around him. The man—or immortal rather —had a heart of gold.

Saleem sighed then looked pointedly at me. "So? Are you going to tell me? Or do I have to force it out of you?"

I grinned. I wanted to say something cheesy like 'ooh, I didn't know you like to play dirty', but the words just didn't seem appropriate spoken seconds before telling him my fucked-up truth.

I sighed and leaned against the pillows behind me. "So . . . I made a trip to Hong Kong."

"Seeing the sights."

"So to speak. High-flying client. Missing kid."

"Explains the fancy duds." He smiled. "Taking the job?"

I nodded. "Yep. Got a little sidetracked there, though."

He raised his eyebrows, his eyes flickering now. I was pretty sure he was losing his cool with me giving him the slow runaround.

Raising my hand, I began to fold over at one finger at a time, ticking my list off as I spoke. "So . . . I was abducted by two thugs. Kicked one of them so hard in the nethers I'm not sure he'd ever have baby-thugs. Was taken to a hotel room across the city by a kitsune of all things—never saw one before so that part was enlightening. Spoke to an Ancient—first time for that too, super interesting. Received the news about the Dark One who will be the cause of the destruction of the world. *And* I was given a few tips on how to identify the spellcaster who bestowed my little poltergeist buddy on me."

Saleem was silent.

I poked him in the shoulder.

He turned to meet my gaze. "Oh? You're done?"

This time I punched him in the bicep.

He didn't react and the gray pallor of his skin confirmed he wasn't taking it well. "This," I threw my hands up in the air, waving them in his face, "*This* is why I don't like telling you stuff."

"This is serious. Mel. You could get hurt."

"Pray tell what do you think I did before you were around?"

"The gargoyle."

I shrugged. "Not like he stayed at my side twenty-four-seven." I leaned toward him. "I can take care of myself. And just because I have a little extra on my plate does not mean you need to forget about your own problems. Transference is not a thing I accept."

Saleem sighed and his eyes grew darker. The whorls on his arms and neck shifted and swam, shadows snaking across his golden skin. Then they stopped moving and faded away as Saleem pulled his glamor back into place. He cocked his head, as if listening for something, then looked around the room. "By the way, where *is* the gargoyle?"

I waved my hands in the air. "No clue. I'm not his keeper. Or his wife."

Saleem gave me an odd look and I burst out laughing. "Men."

"What?" he asked, playing innocent. "I didn't say anything."

"You didn't need to. Just the look on your face is enough."

"What look?" he asked leaning so close his lips almost touched mine, "Oh, you meant the look that says I'm not exactly happy to know someone else might have probably-maybe-once-upon-a-time been my woman's main squeeze."

Then he pushed me back down on the sofa and kissed me, and I forgot the room, forgot all my problems. I even forgot about my evil spirit who was probably enjoying some soft porn viewing right now.

The one thing I did remember made me smile against his mouth.

His woman indeed.

CHAPTER 9

"Will you two please get a damned room? There's a whole bunch to choose from if you move up to the first floor." Steph's unimpressed voice shattered my passion into minuscule pieces, and Saleem and I both sprang apart.

I scrambled for my blouse and bra and ignored the djinn as he buttoned his shirt and pants.

When I turned to glare at her, Steph's expression remained unapologetic. "What? This is the *living* room, ya know," she turned on her heel and walked off saying, "I have info, in case you're interested."

I hurried after her, but not before glancing over my shoulder and sending Saleem a sheepish glance. He winked, and disappeared. And only then did I realize he hadn't told me his reasons for coming in the first place.

Upstairs in the comms room, Steph sank into her chair and tapped the keyboard to pull up a few files on the screen.

"I know it's been ages and you need to get your lady bits oiled once in a while, but please . . . not on the sofa. I watch *TV* on the sofa." Then she stiffened, and swung around to stare at me, "Have you two done this before? On the freaking sofa?"

I sank down beside her, and cupped her face. "I'm sorry Steph, but if you can't tell a make-out session when you see it, then maybe you need a refresher sex-ed class."

She snorted. "Denial won't get you anywhere. You get your groove on all you want. Just keep it off the sofa."

I grinned.

I hadn't missed the small smile at the corner of her mouth, or the way her eyes twinkled. She'd been rooting for Saleem and me for months.

Now, she focused on her keyboard and then pointed at the screen without looking, "This is all I got for the Phaser. And that," she pointed to a larger black screen, "is a record of everything over a period of two years."

The larger flat-screen showed a map of the North American continent, complete with dozens and dozens of little red dots spread out across all the states, from Alaska to Mexico and Cuba.

"He sure was busy," I said, a little in awe. The other screens flashed news articles in slow-mo, photographs of the vigilante from surveillance and witnesses.

"The Phaser is mostly known for saving people using his powers. He stops bank robbers and murderers and wife-beaters. Law enforcement all over the country are happy he's around. The only ones complaining are criminals. And those paid *by* criminals."

I inhaled, studying the almost-endless relay of information. "For a kid, he's impressive."

"You can say that again. He's been incredibly busy over the last two years. Emerged in Chicago, then traveled across the states. There were reports of him in London, Geneva, the Caymans, South Africa and Australia, but he seems to keep regular activity to this continent."

Steph sat back and staring at the screens, biting her lip. "Why are we looking for this guy? Are we apprehending him? Or joining him?"

I sighed. "His mother wants to stop him."

"From doing all the good he does?" she raised her eyebrows, "Selfish bitch."

"Gets worse." I sat on the edge of the desk. "She thinks he's out to sabotage her. That he feels her money is blood money."

Steph lifted a finger. "*Yes*. Elise Garner was once accused of being involved in the blood-diamond trade, even after the accusations against her husband. No evidence ever found. She claimed all her diamonds are from legitimate sources, and from what the press said, she managed to prove it too, because the authorities dropped the case."

"Or were paid to drop it?"

Steph nodded slowly. "Okay, let us say she is guilty. And that her son has a legit reason to damage her financial estate. How will he achieve this?"

I shrugged. "He's a phaser. And a partial teleporter. Manipulates the frequencies of solid objects which allows him to move through metal and stone. My guess is, he'll attempt to deplete her income one step at a time."

I stared at a photo of Erik and his mother standing in front of a Garner's Diamonds store in Milan. "Starting with the diamonds themselves."

Steph was already tapping away as she spoke, "I love the way your mind works." Within seconds she brought up a world map with blue dots that identified cities where Garner's Diamonds had stores. "Twenty sites in total."

"Not as many as I would've expected."

"Nope. But just enough if you want to remain super-exclusive. New York, LA, Chicago, Houston, London, Paris, Rome, Hong Kong. They have reach, so they'd also have pretty tight security."

"Even so, it can't keep *me* out."

"What about Erik?"

I stared at the screen again.

"Why hasn't he attacked her where it hurts. In all the time he's been saving people, helping people, why hasn't he done something substantial about his mother other than a handful of seemingly random breaches?"

I gave a weary sigh as I recognized his pattern. "Because all this time he was assuaging his own guilt, trying to make himself feel better, trying to make amends. And now, finally he wants his own vengeance."

Steph tapped away again, and a photograph of a young boy, his forehead creased as he stared at a chessboard. "This is Erik Garner. Chess-champion at eight, won a scholarship to Yale at twelve, research physicist at a lab after completing his degree at fifteen. Lived at home until he disappeared without a trace."

I frowned. "Impressive. But what changed? What was the catalyst to making him abandon it all?"

"The death of Jeb Garner? Erik was sixteen." Steph enjoyed the thrill of a case that required a little more thinking and strategizing.

"How did he die?" I asked staring at Erik's most recent photo. He looked young for his age, gangly, compensating with a stubbled, longhaired, slouchy look. His gray eyes were piercing bits of silver and it almost felt like he could see through a person's soul.

Steph's voice broke into my thoughts. "Plane went down." Her expression fell. "There's something else."

How much worse can this get?

"My searches on the mother are picking up a trail leading to Sentinel. Files are high-level. Top secret."

I groaned. "Don't tell me the mother is a mage."

"Not sure how relevant that would be to our case," said Steph as her fingers flew across the keyboard.

"It would be pretty relevant. It means she may know about the DarkWorld. It means she may know about *my* abilities. It means she likely knows her son has powers—not suspects as she claims."

Steph swung her chair around and stared at me.

"Which means she's trying to protect more than just her money."

I sighed and stared at the screen showing a photo of Ms Garner's face. Her features were strong, her tan fading, her hair a dark pixie-cut, laugh-lines marking her face.

"You know something, Steph?" She quirked her eyebrow in question. "I have a nagging suspicion that in this particular case we are clueless."

Steph grinned. "Ah. Yeah. *That* was a good movie."

"Shut up, Steph," I said, already out the door as she ran through the highlights of another of her many favorite old movies.

I gritted my teeth and headed to my bathroom.

Knowing what was wrong and being unable to do anything about it was a different kind of hell.

I hated being clueless.

CHAPTER 10

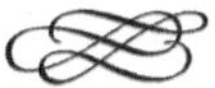

At times like these—when cases are stressful—the days seem to blend together.

Time feels like it doesn't exist much. Add in the jump to Hong Kong and it made time more difficult to assimilate.

It's nothing new though, as the different planes—like the demon realms or the dragon world— also exist within their own time zones, and I've traveled to them enough.

I tossed and turned, sleep hard to obtain. I eventually nodded off to a deep dreamless place of rest from which I awakened acceptably refreshed and a little too oblivious.

Yawning wide and loud, I headed into the bathroom and narrowly missed stepping on the broken shards of glass covering the small rug in front of the washbasin.

I'd been so careful, keeping anything dangerous out of the bathroom, but I'd totally forgotten about the large white glass shade around the above-the-mirror light bulb. Unfortunately for me, the *tokolosje* was an intelligent guy, albeit a very much dead guy. A combination that made my stomach turn.

He was unpredictable, serving up only a slight nosebleed on landing in Hong Kong and one in front of Saleem. I had to wonder if distance from home affected the strength of his hold on me.

I scrounged around in the hall closet for a dustpan and broom, cleaned up the mess and then washed up, my mind on Samuel.

The only way that I was going to get access to him again was to be in the same physical place as his physical body, and for my projected self to be with his projected essence.

Using his body would allow me to gain better access to his essence giving me a stronger feedback while in the ether.

Not only did I need to find Samuel because of Ari, but I also had to do it because Darius required it, because of the Dark One that spelled our doom.

All that end-of-the-world stuff was weighing my shoulders down.

~

After slugging a cup of coffee from the machine in the kitchen, I grabbed my keys and headed out to the truck. The day was gray, the low-hanging clouds burgeoning with a storm.

A flock of blackbirds drew uniformed patterns, dark splotches against a dull blue sky, a second warning of the coming storm.

I put the car in drive, and slid into the street. A glance over my shoulder confirmed that the street was empty of any local law enforcement of the prying kind. Detective Pete Fulbright had been absent of late. After our last encounter a few weeks back— when he'd delivered the news that my client was in the hospital and likely dying—I'd seen very little of him.

Not that I wasn't grateful that he wasn't dogging my every step, it was just strange to look over my shoulder and not see him there.

The thought of Fulbright had my head snapping up. Someone who knew me, that may want to do me harm? Those closest to me, and those who were my enemies.

Could I consider Pete Fulbright, with his decade-long vendetta against me, as a potential spellcaster?

I'd be stupid not to.

I thumped my head against the back of the car seat and considered my next move. How in the holy hell was I supposed to obtain a DNA sample from Fulbright when he'd left me in peace for so long? Surely bumping into him or arranging a meeting with him, could rekindle his desire to stalk me again.

Sucking in a deep breath I decided to take the cowardly way out and ask Saleem to obtain said sample for me. He worked with Fulbright at CPD. I doubt it would be hard for him to get me a strand of hair or a fingernail.

Making a mental note to talk to Saleem as soon as I got back from Samuel's, I tried to shut it out of my mind for the moment. I rolled down the window, inhaling the electric bite of the air and drove off.

Parking outside Samuel's old antebellum mansion, I stared up at the curtain that shaded his room. The white drape billowed in a sudden gust of wind, reminding me that the storm was going to come sooner than I'd expected.

I locked the car and hurried to the front door, using my key to let myself in. Thankfully, Samuel's niece was otherwise employed and we'd ended up hiring a caregiver for him instead. It felt rather peaceful not to be bombarded with sarcasm and biting criticism before I met with him.

As I bounded up the stairs—a habit my mom had tried and failed to rid me of—my foot slipped and I almost tripped.

"Fuck," I caught myself just before I cracked my forehead open on the edge of the top stair, remembering too late that the damned *tokolosje* was still around.

Guess if I killed myself before the poltergeist did, then technically I'd win.

Idiot.

I got to my feet, took a deep breath and waited until my heartbeat returned to something near normal.

I straightened my spine, took another breath, then headed toward Samuel's room, where I stood on the threshold for a moment. Samuel sat in the rocking chair at the table beside the window.

To an onlooker, he'd appear to be staring out at the view of the expansive grounds of the estate.

My stomach twinged knowing he wasn't seeing a damned thing.

I drew closer and set my bag on the floor before taking a seat in the chair opposite Samuel. The table held a glass vase bearing three drooping daffodils, and an empty teacup.

Poor Samuel.

I was pretty certain he wouldn't have been able to drink that on his own.

Ever since he'd fallen into this catatonic state, we'd had to spoon-feed him everything. Technically, he belonged in a full-time care facility, but since he still retained breathing and cardiac function, his family wanted him kept at home. Like me, they still waited for the day that he would return to us, the day he'd open his eyes, and give us that bright smile he reserved for those he loved.

I leaned closer and took his hand in mine, feeling the press of his bones through thin, fleshless skin. I spoke to him, soft words, reassuring him more on the off-chance that he could somehow still hear me.

He'd woken a few times, once to give me a message that sent me searching for him. And finding him lurking in a different plane.

Samuel was lost in a permanent projection, physically in two places at the same time. And until he fulfilled whatever goal he sought, he wasn't about to come back home. My deepest fear was that he'd return too late, because his poor frail body was beginning to fail him.

Holding his hand, I settled against the backrest and sank into the ether.

Samuel's biofeedback was confusing. It seemed to be pushing me in two separate directions. One back toward his unconscious body, and then in an entirely new one.

The different worlds, the various planes and realms that comprised the DarkWorld, existed not side-by-side, but almost in the same place at the same time. I'd never understood the dynamics of time and the different worlds, but I'd never needed to. Because traveling through the ether had distilled the confusion for me, into a semblance of sense that I'd accepted a long time ago.

But right now, I encountered a sense of a new and unusual presence, a tether to the feedback that made my stomach tighten.

This time, I didn't speed along attached to Samuel's feedback. Instead I moved slowly, carefully, a deep sense of anxiety making me expect something to go wrong at any moment.

The further along I went, the stronger the sense of unease grew, until I finally reached the location in the Veil where the ether met a different plane. A world to which Samuel's feedback beckoned.

Still keeping a tight hold on the essence that guided me to Samuel, I slipped through the gap in the Veil and projected into a cave.

One of the strangest caves I'd ever been in, the ground was covered in red dirt, and the walls constructed of red crystal.

Flickering lights emanated from crevices and narrow ledges all along the length of the tunnel, and I squinted at them, looking closer.

Someone dropped oil and wicks into convenient little wells

made by the projecting crystals. The lights only served to make the tunnel more eerie, with its red glow casting demonic shadows in front of me.

Footsteps pounded along the tunnel floor and two uniformed men hurried toward me. They wore dark leather pants and close-fitting leather jackets. I frowned at the construction of the garments, noting there was no continuous piece of fabric to be found. Both articles of clothing were constructed of irregular-sized pieces of leather stitched together haphazardly with thick twine. I frowned, but dismissed their fashion sense for the moment and focused on the men themselves.

Jagged curved blades jutted from scabbards at each of their hips, and the sight of their faces would likely haunt my night-mares for weeks to come. Not that I was new to demons—having seen my fair share—but these two were positively monstrous.

With their long canines, and yellow horns erupting from tufts of hair on each of their bald heads, they looked like something straight out of Dante's Inferno. I shifted aside—more instinct because I was only projecting and there was no way they'd have seen me—and studied them for weaknesses as they passed.

I could see none.

Giant muscles in both arms and legs, stern and unrelenting expressions on their faces, they both looked terrifying enough that if confronted with an army of these creatures I wouldn't be surprised if most people laid down their swords, or turned and ran.

I headed in the opposite direction, keeping an eye out for more soldiers. A low rumbling echoed in my direction and at first I thought it was conversation.

But as I drew closer I recognized the sound of drunken singing and raucous laughter. Within this strange and night-marish place, someone was having a lot of fun.

But the place itself was irrelevant.

Samuel was my goal.

CHAPTER 11

*H*is biofeedback throbbed within my grip, much stronger now. He must be close for his energy to be almost tangible against my senses.

I hurried along, following the feedback so fast I'd glided swiftly past a large doorway before finding myself turned around by the pull of his power.

It crackled within my grasp, tugging me toward the entrance to a large hall filled with soldiers; eating, drinking and fighting according to their personal preferences.

I paused on the threshold and studied the demons gathered inside, seated on chairs eating, laughing, and even throwing food at each other. Along the left wall, a line of soldiers stood at attention. The one closest to me turned to look straight at my face.

The recognition in his eyes sent a flash of cold fear down the back of my spine.

Had he seen me?

I remained as still as possible and watched him as he stared back at me. Frowning, I concentrated on his eyes, reluctantly admitting that he was familiar to me.

Samuel's biofeedback pulsed against my touch, and I took a step into the room feeling it pull me in the direction of the guard.

He stared at me with an intensity that lifted the hair on the back of my neck.

I stepped further into the room, but he stiffened and shook his head slightly, giving me a warning glare.

I frowned. Why would one of the demons be warning me off?

I stood transfixed, as it hit me.

Samuel?

Was it possible that Samuel was the guard I was wasting precious time gaping at?

As with all the other soldiers, he was dressed in patchwork leather, and wore a sword at his waist. The only difference with him was his face was covered in a patchwork leather helmet, with a ragged pair of holes for his eyes.

Before I could think of anything further, the sound of boot-heels thudding on the stone floor had me spinning on my heel.

A cloaked hooded figure walked toward me, right in my path of escape. Stepping back, I assessed my situation. I had nowhere to go, and at least one of the four in the entourage was going to end up walking through me.

I froze in place mentally shutting my eyes as the cloaked man strode right into my ethereal presence.

Pain slammed into me, slicing into my brain and scraping down my spine. Every muscle in my body tightened with agony. The only thing I could be thankful for was the figure in the cloak hadn't stopped until he'd walked right through me.

But, something must have alerted him, because as I looked over my shoulder he stopped in his tracks and turned around, staring at the spot where I stood. I still couldn't see his face, but from the shape of his jaw and mouth I suspected this person was human. Or at least part-human.

A very effeminate jaw and mouth.

Which could mean nothing.

I watched as he faced me, his body tense. Over his shoulder I could see the masked guard watching me, fear in his eyes. He was shaking his head left to right, his eyes narrowed as if he was urging me to do something.

I knew what he was trying to say.

Leave. Leave now.

I took a step back, caring little that I'd pass through the man's guards. I was just too desperate to get away. The pain hadn't receded yet. In fact, my body resounded with agony, the intensity now multiplied tenfold.

The pain was so excruciating that I sucked in a breath, and felt my knees fold beneath me. I blinked.

This wasn't supposed to happen.

Never before had I gained any form of solidity while projecting to alternate planes or realms. My gut churned with fear, and as the black spots creeping into the corners of my vision confirmed I was going to pass out.

And I couldn't do a damn thing about it. The last thing I saw before I sank into oblivion was the masked guard staring at me, sadness in his eyes.

I knew those eyes had been familiar.

Samuel.

～

I woke up slumped over, the side of my face sore, wondering what had just happened.

My head lay on the table and my spine hurt from being crouched over for too long. I lifted my head and straightened slowly, silencing a cry of pain as my back cracked.

Samuel still sat in the same position as when I'd left, staring unseeing out of the window.

I massaged a sore spot on my cheek. I must have hit it on the table when I'd passed out. What a strange experience.

First the masked man warning me to leave, then the cloaked figure behaving as if he'd seen me, and most importantly the pain; so intense it had knocked me out.

I thought about the masked soldier, his face hidden, but his eyes so familiar. Eyes that belonged to Samuel.

This whole debacle needed further investigation. Next time I entered this demon realm, I'd have to be much more careful.

And definitely a hell of a lot smarter.

Samuel was in the demon realm, a guard within the ranks of demons. Was that why he kept his face hidden? Or did they know he was human and tolerated him? And why did he warn me off? Surely he knew nobody could see me.

And yet, the hooded figure had reacted as if he'd sensed my presence. That was not supposed to happen.

I spent a few more minutes with Samuel, bringing him up to date on my most recent case. It always felt good to talk to him, even when I knew there was no chance of him responding. Still better than talking to his gravestone.

I fell silent for a moment, feeling the weight of guilt press down on me as I readied myself to betray Samuel. I withdrew a plastic Ziploc bag and a tweezer from my pocket, and proceeded to grab a hair sample from my mentor's head. His hair was brittle and broke as the metal teeth of the tweezer closed onto them.

After a few tries, I spied a strand on his shoulder and retrieved it carefully. My heart thumped, not from worry that I may get caught, but rather from the guilt overwhelming me. I took a breath and sealed the plastic bag before depositing it in my jacket pocket.

I scooped up the empty cup and grabbed my satchel from the floor, then headed back downstairs. Depositing the cup into the kitchen I spoke to Clara, the bubbly blonde nurse, to get caught up on Samuel's condition. Despite her cheerful smile, I could see the worry in her eyes.

A few minutes later I was driving back home, the giant hollow in my gut screaming at me. Time was getting dangerously short for Samuel.

And for Ari.

CHAPTER 12

*A*fter the trauma of being so close to Samuel and being unable to reach him, plus the fact that I'd encountered someone who could sense me in the ether, I felt a little off balance.

Often, I'd turn to Drake, but in his absence, I felt myself needing to see Storm. He'd been busy lately, dealing with new kids no doubt. The man had a heart of gold, and I personally owed him a great deal.

I wasn't sure where I'd have ended up without his guidance and mentorship.

Plus, I had him to thank for Drake and Steph and even Natasha. Not to mention Tara, my Fae MetalSinger friend

Unfortunately Tara, who would have been on my shoulder-to-cry-on list, was also not around to help me out.

I pulled myself from my woe-is-me mode and projected to Storm's office. Thankfully he was there, though he did look a little preoccupied, pacing in front of his desk.

Jumping to the hall outside his office, I knocked on his door. The sound of pacing stopped and Storm called out. "Come in."

I headed inside, closing the door behind me. "Hey, you have a minute?"

He smiled, but the cheer wasn't reflected in his eyes. "Sure. Come on in. I have a few minutes, but I have another appointment soon."

I smiled. "I won't take too much of your time." He waved me to one of the armchairs, but remained leaning against the side of his desk. As I sat there, trying to form the words, I realized how little there was that I *could* share with Storm.

There was so much about Samuel and me that he didn't know. And he had no idea that Ari was still alive because I'd been afraid to tell anyone in case I was wrong.

And of course, Storm had no idea I was as powerful a teleporter and astral projector as I was. That secret had been at Samuel's insistence for my own protection.

And now Darius and the Dark One could be added to my mountain of secrets that I'd slowly begun to keep from Storm.

So, instead of looking for advice, I decided I'd be just a friend visiting a friend.

I could do that.

I gave him a cheery smile. "Thought I'd check up on you. See how things are going?"

Storm's smile was more forced than ever, the usually bright blue of his eyes a murky navy. "I'm fine, Melisande. Was there something urgent you needed?"

I shook my head. "I was just in the area."

Storm tilted his head to look at me. "How have *you* been, Mel?" he asked, suddenly turning the tables on me.

He seemed genuinely interested, which was Storm's way.

I forced a smile on my face. "I'm fine."

"You don't look fine." He leaned closer, inspecting my face. "In fact, you look a little pale, and gray around the gills."

I let out a sharp laugh. A resident evil would do that to you.

But I didn't say that aloud.

Waving him off, I said, "No. I'm fine. Just a little tired with so many jumps and back to back cases."

"Oh?" I could have sworn he looked a little disappointed, but then his face was inscrutable again.

I pushed to my feet and gave him a smile. "I won't take up any more of your time." I felt more off balance now than before I'd arrived.

Storm's odd behavior had me questioning myself all over again.

As I opened the door, Storm said, "Mel?"

I turned to look at him over my shoulder.

"Take care of yourself, okay?" his eyes glittered and I couldn't define the look he gave me. I could have sworn it was satisfaction—perhaps because he knew he'd succeeded after all these years of mentorship.

I couldn't argue that he deserved the satisfaction.

CHAPTER 13

*D*riving back home my mental note to talk to Saleem regarding Fulbright popped into my head like an alarm, something that rarely happened.

Showed how this whole situation was bugging the shit out of me.

The thought of the sexy djinn reminded me that we had unfinished business. He'd left so fast that he'd failed to update me on his mission. And I had a favor to ask.

It was time that we talked.

Before he did anything drastic without checking in with me.

I sent Saleem a short text telling him I needed to see him.

Our relationship was far from needy, so an admission on my part would have him over fast. But only because he'd be worried.

Returning home, I hurried straight upstairs with my stolen sample of Samuel's fragile hair. I threw my keys on my night-stand and dropped my satchel beside the bed. Behind my head-board was a moveable panel, which hid a little cubby hole. I'd hidden all sorts of things inside the secret space over the years.

Stolen DNA samples were a first.

Then I changed into yoga pants and a loose tee, and slipped on a ragged pair of slippers before making a quick call to Darius.

For an immortal he was pretty onto it in terms of modern tech. He answered the video call and I found myself staring at his hooded form as he faced the camera.

When Tanaka had instructed me to video-call the ancient directly I'd been more than surprised. And now, my stomach was a bundle of nerves.

The ancients were so respected I somehow felt that the video-call was all kinds of wrong.

But he smiled and drew closer to the screen. "Melisande. You have news?" he asked. His eyes were still hidden.

Taking a deep breath, I changed the subject, tired of thinking about my lack of judgment.

"I tried to contact Samuel and I encountered something really worrying."

My voice must have held an edge to it. Darius's smile disappeared and he asked, "What happened?" His tone was kind and patient and comforted me somewhat.

I proceeded to give him a detailed account of my projection into the strange red underworld and my encounter with the hooded figure.

Though I couldn't make out Darius's full expression I got the sense that he was concerned. "Melisande, I do think you need to get well, and do so quickly. There is a possibility that your weakness could mean you may not be strong enough to withstand this person's power and save Samuel."

Or Ari.

I nodded. "So how do I find this spellcaster."

"The magic would have been cast using blood. So the key to understanding who he is, is to use your blood to track him."

"Can I track him?"

"It's possible. You will only know if you try."

I nodded and rang off, and while I waited for Saleem's

response I pulled out onions, carrots and celery, and threw a tray of ground beef into the microwave to defrost. I was always in a rush, jumping here, projecting there, helping someone out, and saving someone else.

I hardly ever had time to relax or just not do anything urgent, and right now I felt like I was in limbo.

I chopped vegetables for what Mom said was a Mirepoix. As young as I'd been, Mom had insisted I learn to find my way around a kitchen, and to enjoy myself while I did it.

"Never dislike the cooking process, Melly. Because cooking is creation and it's the only time you can be a goddess in your own world."

If only I could find more time to do these creationist things. Instead, I chopped onions, carrots in varying sizes, and forgot to remove the strings on the celery before I gave them the same treatment.

Before long, a Bolognese sauce was bubbling on the stove, while a second deeper pot was slowly coming to the boil for the pasta. I was struggling to keep my eyes open, but I had to eat more than I needed to sleep, and sometimes cooking helped me think.

I'd realized a while ago that I hadn't been sleeping well and I wondered if that was a side effect of the evil creep. Even my eating patterns had been thrown off-kilter. Sometimes, no matter how tired I was, I'd ignore the need to sleep and rush off to do something that needed doing.

There was only one of me after all.

I stared at the empty kitchen, missing Drake's presence in front of the stove. I wasn't sure how long it would be before he returned.

If he returned.

Stop it Mel. It doesn't help to be negative.

I bit my lip. Drake was going be so mad that I hadn't told him about the poltergeist. That I hadn't asked him for help. But I couldn't keep him here when he needed to go home.

I'd watched him struggle with the decision for months, seeing his eyes, the way they had darkened at the mention of his family. I just prayed that he'd get the resolution he needed from them.

And from his father.

My attempt to find Samuel had failed. We were still waiting for Erik-possibly-the-Phaser to make his move, but at least now I could concentrate on the spellcaster who had saddled me with the creepy poltergeist.

Bastard.

I felt a surge of pure hatred at the person who'd cursed me. I just could not understand who would do such a thing. Not that I couldn't understand someone hating me.

I'd done enough to ruin the lives of some pretty bad people, but whoever had cursed me with the evil spirit, with hobbling my powers, with nosebleeds and dizziness and certain death, whoever this person was, he was one malicious son of a bitch.

I'd just set the pot of pasta in the middle of the table when Saleem materialized beside me. He smiled at me through the haze of burnt-orange and gold embers, and my stomach tightened.

We'd been through so damned much in the last few weeks, and hadn't had much chance to indulge our affection—or our attraction—to our satisfaction.

Not yet.

And that incident on the couch earlier so did not count.

CHAPTER 14

Saleem opened his arms and I went to him, enjoying the comfort of feeling his body against mine, his arms wrapped tightly around me. In his arms, I'd found a safe harbor, some semblance of peace. Even if it only lasted for a brief moment.

"You okay?" he whispered in my ear, his breath warm against my skin.

I nodded, my forehead brushing his chest, finding my current position all too comfortable.

A chuckle rumbled in his chest, vibrating into my cheek. "Liar."

"Yeah," I mumbled. Taking a deep breath, I straightened and pushed my hair behind my ears. Then I pointed at the pot. "Food?"

He quirked an eyebrow. "*You* cooked?"

I glared at him. "What the hell does that mean?"

With a shrug he sat down and reached for the pot lid. "I dunno. Just thought with the gargoyle gone you'd be dining on takeout."

I grunted and tugged open the refrigerator door, retrieving a bottle of sauvignon blanc. I set it on the table, then grabbed wine glasses from the cupboard above the fridge. "Here. You need the fortification."

"What for?" he asked as he loaded plates with pasta and stuck a fork in each pile of goodness, handing me one as I took a seat.

"Your battle plan for going home." I shoved a forkful of pasta into my mouth, cursing myself for having to lie to him. His mother's words still rang in my head. Saleem had to get his plan together and get himself to the djinn world asap.

He nodded as he swallowed. "The gargoyle leaving has put a spanner in the works. I'm short an operative, now."

"Yeah." A pang of sadness stabbed me in the heart. "Wish he were here but we can't dwell on that. You need to find someone else to help you."

He shook his head. "I don't want to bring anyone else into this. It could be dangerous."

I gave an inelegant snort. "You can't go by yourself." When he shifted his gaze from my face to his plate, I recognized the movement—avoidance. I reached out and tugged the sleeve of his shirt. "Hey. Call Logan. Tell him what you're planning. He'll want to help you."

Saleem shook his head.

I sighed and put my fork down slowly. "If I were Logan, I'd be supremely pissed off that you didn't ask me for my help, especially since we're such good friends." He looked up, flames flickering in the depths of his eyes as I continued, "and especially since you've helped me out on so many occasions."

He exhaled harshly. "You know I don't like making my problems other peoples' problems."

I rolled my eyes. The guy was too damned stubborn. "Logan isn't *other people*. Think of him as family . . . if it will make you feel better."

Saleem proceeded to shovel food into his mouth—more

avoidance behavior—but I knew he was thinking it over. Probably looking for holes in my theory.

I hoped he wouldn't find any.

At last, after a silence so tense I could have cut through it with a knife, he nodded. "Okay. I'll tell him."

"Please do. Or I will."

He narrowed his gaze at me. "Why are you beginning to sound like my mother?" he asked, a smile lifting the corner of his mouth.

My stomach twinged, but I stuck my tongue out at him and grinned, hiding my guilt as best as I could. Saleem was oblivious, but I knew I'd pay for all these lies one day. I just hoped—coward that I was—that it wouldn't be soon.

"So, can you do me a favor?" I asked, desperately needing to fill the silence, because suddenly the only thing I could hear was our breath and the sound of food being chewed and swallowed.

Weird.

He nodded almost absently, and I took a deep breath. "I need to obtain DNA samples from all possible suspects in my poltergeist investigation."

He offered a nod and a quirk of an inquisitive eyebrow, his gaze on his plate.

"So . . . I was thinking Fulbright was a legitimate suspect."

Saleem looked up. "I'd put him on the list for sure."

I nodded. "So . . . since I need his DNA—a strand of hair will do—I was hoping you'd be kind enough to pick up a sample for me."

He grinned. "You make it sound like Fulbright takeout."

"Shudder," I said as I shuddered.

"Don't worry. I'll get it for you." Saleem nodded, more serious now. "Have you made a list of suspects?"

I didn't answer, and as he continued to eat I got the feeling he understood that betraying my closest friends wasn't something that I wanted to discuss.

Fulbright was okay since he was as far from a friend as possible.

I sucked in a breath, and in an attempt to steer the conversation in a different direction, I told him about the Elite.

He lifted an eyebrow. "I knew they'd contact you."

"How so?"

"They're headhunting. Kai, you, Logan. Me. I'm not sure who else, but I can guess if you're a talented mage you're gonna get the call."

I sighed and finished my last bite. "I just hope this isn't going to be another Omega."

Saleem shook his head, getting to his feet. He reached for my plate and stacked it on top of his. "I don't believe so. The Elite is being spearheaded by the Ancients and the Supreme High Council. That's a lot of legitimate power right there. Omega on the other hand started out as a rebellion against Sentinel."

I nodded and Saleem got to his feet, taking the dishes to the sink. Sentinel had been the only organization that stood for policing the paranormals worldwide. Initiated by the Supreme High Council more than four hundred years ago, they'd once been the only law enforcement authority for the paranormal world.

Then a small faction of people broke away and began Omega. Until now, any association with Omega wasn't seen in a negative light since the High Council had long since accepted the status quo. Omega, over the decades, had evolved into a different, more legitimate agency.

Saleem sighed, the sound muffled as he reached beneath the sink cupboard for washing liquid. "The walls Omega have built over the years are fast crumbling. Agents are seeking asylum with Sentinel left, right, and center."

"Not that it's their fault what Omega was doing." I got up and cleared the table, wiped it down, and began to dry the dishes as he washed and rinsed.

How very domestic.

Saleem shrugged again.

"So do you have a team ready?"

He nodded.

"Am I on it?" Until now, we hadn't really discussed the details of his plan. I'd been reluctant to ask too many questions considering the Djinn queen had asked that I stay out of the mission.

"Definitely not."

"Why?" I asked, my voice rising an octave.

"Do you even need to ask?"

I pouted, annoyed that my stupid poltergeist was beginning to spoil more than just my jumping. But Saleem had a point. I couldn't go traipsing around Mithras and then come back to EarthWorld missions and expect to survive the kind of nosebleeds that would incur.

Not until this spirit was exorcised.

Saleem's expression softened. "Besides, it's only recon now. For all we know, I won't be able to do a thing about Riz."

Saleem reached for a tea towel to wipe his hands dry. He'd scrubbed the sink down and it gleamed, which it ought to considering he'd done such a damned good job.

I had to admit I was impressed with his kitchen skills.

I cleared my throat, "So about that DNA-takeout run . . ." Saleem wasn't exactly Fulbright's favorite person. Not since having been forced to work with him.

"Mmh?" Saleem asked, dropping the towel on the counter behind him.

"Just don't get caught, okay?"

"Yes, ma'am."

He tapped his temple with two fingers, winked and then disappeared in a flurry of bronze and black swirling dust.

CHAPTER 15

The next morning, I headed back downstairs. The smell of bacon and eggs wafted out into the hall and the sounds of Steph in the kitchen with her dub-step music drew a smile to my lips. At least some things had remained the same.

I jogged down the stairs, entranced by the prospect of food, and stepped on the nail jutting out of the carpet two steps down.

Pain stabbed through the heel of my foot, and I let out a scream as I lost my balance and tumbled down the remaining dozen stairs.

I rolled myself into a ball keeping all limbs safely tucked close. It didn't save me from almost breaking my neck, or knocking my elbows and knees as I landed on the hall floor.

Nor did it stop me from leaving a glaring trail of blood in my wake.

I glanced at my bare foot, covered in blood and throbbing with pain. A gory hole on the top of my foot glared back at me. The bottom of my foot ached with equal intensity, confirming what I could see.

Through and through.

Steph raced into the hall, yelling loudly, "What the hell, Mel.

Are you okay?" She sank down beside me, reaching out to check my forehead.

I brushed her hand off. "I don't have a fever, Steph." I unraveled myself and sat up, testing the back of my head. "A hole in my foot, yes. Fever, no." My fingers grazed a small bump that promised to grow much larger very soon.

I knew I was snapping but she didn't seem to notice as she checked me for damages and positioned herself at my feet.

"Holy shitballs, Mel. There's a hole in your foot."

Even though I wanted to roll my eyes, I couldn't. "Wow. Your powers of perception are incomparable."

She rolled her own eyes and shot to her feet, racing to the kitchen so fast I wondered if she was a mage and hadn't told us. "Don't move," she yelled as she rummaged in the drawer.

Another eye-roll moment, but I restrained myself.

I rolled onto my knees, got up onto my good foot, and hopped to the living room. The sofa would feel much better than the hardwood floor, especially with all the places I currently hurt.

"Don't worry. I'm not moving," I lied, "I don't plan on breaking anything else." As I sat, I shifted my head and felt a bolt of pain slam its way into my head. Taking a careful breath, I resolved to remain still—at least for a while.

"I didn't mean you," she yelled, "we don't need any more damage to the carpets. Bloodstains don't come off easily."

I hid a smile as I shook my head, then winced. Steph sped to the stairs, growled when she saw I wasn't there, then raced into the living room moving so fast she had to skid to a stop to avoid tumbling onto me. Her arms were loaded with bandages, bottles and a hot towel.

"I'll fix you right up." She spoke confidently, but her voice wavered enough that I knew she was being brave.

"Before you do, be a darling and call for Chloe." The tension within my body roiled and my teeth began to chatter.

Steph nodded, then placed the back of her fingers on my forehead. "You're cold and a little moist. Probably shock. One order of Dr Chloe coming up."

Steph scrambled around for my phone, which I'd thrown clear across the hall as I'd fallen. She dialed quickly and got Chloe who agreed to come over fast.

Then she set to work, fixing my foot up with disinfectant and antibacterial cream and bandages. Everything I knew a mage doctor would resolve soon enough, but I let her do it only because she was Steph, and because I'd noticed how her hands had shivered as she'd reached for the bandages, and how her voice rose that much higher as she scolded every time I'd moved.

Steph was in as much shock as I was.

Ten minutes later, while Steph had left to make me a cup of hot tea, the doorbell went. With the kettle going, she didn't hear the doorbell so I hopped off the sofa and limped to the door. Through the glass I saw Chloe and a boy who looked about sixteen.

As I opened the door, the boy said, "Call me when you need me, Doctor Chloe." Then he teleported off the front porch.

I raised my eyebrows. "Very talented for his age."

Chloe chuckled as she entered the room. "That's nothing. You should have seen Logan at twelve. Now *he* was a force to be reckoned with."

I nodded and limped back into the living room, with Chloe walking beside me, her expression concerned. I sat slowly. "Can you explain what just happened?" There was the mother-hen Chloe that I knew and loved.

I shrugged. "Nothing fancy. I just fell down the stairs," I looked away, feeling stupid.

"And you didn't think to teleport out of there and save yourself the fall."

"There wasn't any time. I only fell from halfway down."

Chloe glared at me. "How *did* you fall?"

"She stepped on a nail."

Chloe looked confused until Steph—who'd walked in with a small tray bearing a teapot, a mug, sugar, and milk—handed her a plastic bag containing a bloody nail. "That's the culprit, although I'm not entirely sure how it came loose enough to embed itself so deep into her foot."

"How deep?" Chloe took the plastic bag and stared so hard at the nail that she almost looked cross-eyed.

"Right through and out the top of her instep."

I felt dizzy just thinking about it.

Chloe was pale as she turned to look at me.

"Chloe. I need you, so please don't pass out on me."

"I'm not going to pass out. I'm not some fragile female, you silly girl." She set the packet on the coffee table and sat beside me, taking my hand in hers as Steph mixed too much sugar into my tea.

Slowly, Chloe's magic worked as she drew the tension and the pain out of my body. Chloe wasn't a true med-mage, only having the power to absorb excess emotions.

On the same wavelength as me, Chloe was already reaching for her phone and dialing someone, leaving a brisk message.

When she cut the call, she said, "You need a med-mage to take the pain away and heal your foot. I'd like to avoid any infection and you need the rapid healing."

Although my instinct was to decline politely and then suffer it out on my own, the other two women in the room were staring at me, their eyes so filled with emotion I knew I'd have a tough time explaining myself away.

I nodded and settled back, letting her do her work. While she eased my tension, I wondered what I was going to do now. I still had to find the person who cursed me. Studying Chloe now, I cursed the fact that she was also on my list. But Darius had said it could be anyone.

I just couldn't trust anyone, no matter who they were.

Hot tears welled up in my eyes as I reached behind Chloe

with my free hand and picked two strands of gray hair from the shoulder of her coat. She'd been so concerned with me, she hadn't remembered to remove it.

I held them at the tips between two fingernails and slipped them into my pocket before leaning against the backrest.

I hadn't remembered to get a sample from Drake and made a note to check his bathroom. Just the thought of knowing that I had to collect evidence from my friends made me feel sick, but it was for everyone's safety that I had to do it. It wasn't as if I could call them all to one place and ask them for samples. It was way more complicated than that.

Besides, it was my burden to bear. If the guilty person was outed in full view of everyone else, it meant that they'd all be in danger from the spellcaster.

I had to work smart.

Find the spellcaster, find the witchdoctor.

CHAPTER 16

Chloe did her calming thing, after which a rather stern, too-quiet Dr Niall arrived to treat my injuries. Blond and lanky, he could have been Steph's twin, but he barely looked left or right after he'd arrived.

He'd tended to my injury, knitting the wound from inside and then sealing the entrance and exit wounds both with magic and some kind of clear gel bandage.

He left me with a bottle of pills for the pain.

Some bedside manner.

Chloe departed with the *friendly* doctor and Steph helped me up to bed where, despite my denial of fatigue, I fell asleep within minutes.

I woke an hour later, enjoying a brief moment of peace. And then, when I felt a dribble of hot moistness on my cheek I remembered the craptastic life I was living.

Another freaking nosebleed.

Resolutely, I grabbed the Kleenex from my nightstand and cleaned my nose up. Shimmying out of bed, I tested my foot and found I could walk well enough, except for a few twinges when I put my full weight on it.

I limped out of the room and headed down the hall to Drake's room. He'd left without even a note but I was used to that. We'd never babysat each other, so I hadn't expected a touching farewell.

I crossed his silent room and entered the darkened bathroom. Drake was almost OCD and his bathroom was meticulously clean. I felt awful rummaging inside his trash can but I had to. It was in order to rule him out.

Despite the necessity, my words rang hollow.

Deep within the trash I found discarded floss—because apparently the gargoyle was obsessive about his teeth—as well as fingernail clippings. I bagged them both, cursed my reflection as I got to my feet, and then returned to my room and hid the bags.

After changing, I went in search of Steph and found her bedroom empty. She was probably up in the comms center which gave me ample time to grab a few strands of her hair off her hairbrush and deposit them in my secret hiding place.

That's five down.

And a bunch more to go.

The more I did this, the worse I felt about myself.

Thankfully, I hadn't needed to deliberately obtain a sample from Saleem. All that hot and heavy petting had left behind sufficient hair samples to test.

What would Saleem think?

Not only was I lying to him about his mother, but I was now also going behind his back and stealing DNA samples from him.

He knew about my search for DNA, but I hadn't asked him for a donation of his own. Instead I was skulking around, stealing DNA samples from the people I cared about.

I had a pretty good idea this was strike two.

The kitchen was empty except for a pot of coffee with a sticky-note on it saying 'drink me', and a bowl of cookies marked 'eat me'.

Smiling, I ate then headed outside. My intention was to head out to see Natasha. The drive out to her place was always calming, and despite my impatience to get there, it managed to make me feel so much better.

I'd woken with another nosebleed and decided no more jumps until I was sure it was necessary.

I grabbed the keys to Steph's car and headed out to see Natasha. I'd parked the truck off only because Drake—the only one who knew how to coax the hunk of junk to life—was no longer around.

Steph's electric two-person car was the type of vehicle you encountered where the first question out of your mouth would be 'where's the rest of it?'.

Drake called it Steph's Mini-Skirt.

I slid into the car, feeling the metal, glass and leather close in on me. The vehicle was too small, but I had little choice. As much as I'd love to be stubborn about it, I could not deny that my health was questionable.

I could be careless if it was just me. But endangering my health meant, unfortunately, endangering the lives of those around me.

I'd texted Natasha but received no answer so I figured I'd drive over anyway. If she wasn't home, I'd go out to her pond—her very magical and calming pond—and enjoy a little peace and quiet.

Things had been far too crazy lately.

What with Erik and his concerned mother, Samuel and the strange demon realm he was hiding in, and the hooded figure so powerful he could almost sense me even in projection mode. And Saleem and Drake both dealing with family drama.

And the Dark One—whoever she was—and now the hunt for my own personal stalker-killer.

Could it even get any worse than this?

As I drove out of the city limits, I passed miles of dried and barren cornfields, until I reached the edge of the wasteland.

Going to Natasha's was almost a magical journey, like crossing over from a land of devastation and drought to one of bounty and plenty.

Past Natasha's protective ward nature thrived, encapsulated by her magic, protected from drought and plague and death. Much of what her land produced went to supplement the education and needs of the kids Storm looked after. Natasha saw it as her way of contributing, of giving something back, of supporting Storm in his endeavor to give the lost and the lonely a second chance.

I sighed.

Storm was another name on my list. And he was one I did not relish the thought of meeting with subterfuge on my mind. I knew he was immortal, but you never could tell whether they could see through humanity's failings and identify the lies beneath the faces we showed to the world.

Storm had always understood me, had all too often just told me what my issues were and how to deal with them. It had been hard at first. Until I understood his intentions were only for my own good.

The man had his heart in the right place and I hoped that he'd stick around for a long time. The paranormal kids of Chicago needed him way too much.

My thoughts wandered to how far I'd come since that fateful night when I'd lost everything in one sweeping moment of bloody destruction, that moment when the end of everything I loved had culminated in the beginning of everything I now couldn't live without.

Two sides of a life lived only half as much as it should have been.

CHAPTER 17

The clouds hung low over the flat countryside, and the sun-splashed ruby, tangerine, and purple into the shimmering sky. The beauty of the late morning sky set my mood to melancholy, a state I disliked.

Melancholy brought up memories I'd rather not recall, regrets I'd rather not relive.

I shook the thoughts off and drove with the window down, inhaling the cool air outside, enjoying the serenity of a moment without pain or pressure or persecution.

When I drew up in front of Natasha's house, I felt calmer than I'd been for a long while. Perhaps the decision not to teleport here was smarter than I'd expected.

As I climbed out of the car and shut the door, Natasha appeared from the woods beyond the house, accompanied by a chorus of cicadas chirping their song. She carried a wooden pail filled with water, and her body seemed to glow in the golden light.

Her bright pink kaftan should have clashed with her white hair. Instead, they coexisted in beautiful harmony.

Must be witch magic.

She gave me a bright smile as she headed up the porch steps and placed the pail on the floor beside the door.

"Hey you," she wiped her hands on her kaftan and met me at the top stair for a hug.

Natasha was, and always would be, the sister I never had. I'd found I could tell her anything and apart from Saleem, she was the only one who knew about the poltergeist.

Which made me feel worse as I considered the ways and means to obtain a hair sample from her. I knew how the wooden horse must have felt when Troy was infiltrated.

What the hell are you thinking, Mel?

"How are you," Natasha patted my arm, bringing me out of my thought, "You look like shit."

"Thanks," I grimaced and poked a finger into her shoulder. "Is today I'm-not-answering-my-phone day?"

Natasha's lips twisted into a grimace. "Sorry."

As she turned to enter the house I said, "You didn't answer. I could have been dead by now."

She shrugged. "I'd just bring you back from the dead," she deadpanned.

Snorting, I closed the door and followed her into the large flagstone kitchen. It felt odd being here without Drake. The gargoyle had often insisted on driving me to Natasha's, and in the beginning, I'd assumed the two of them didn't get along.

So not true.

They were now a sort-of couple.

If that could be possible considering he'd left the EarthWorld for his home plane.

I plonked myself onto a chair at her kitchen table and watched as she poured a bright red drink into a glass. "So I need some help tracking someone down."

She lifted an eyebrow as she set the glass before me. "Forgive me for the confusion, but I was under the impression that *you* are the tracker."

Letting out a huff of air, I lifted the glass and sipped. After swallowing the sweet rich cherry juice, I said, "I'm looking for a very special kind of kitsune."

Natasha returned to the table with her own glass and took a seat beside me. "Not many kitsunes around. They tend to keep to themselves."

Darkness encroached as black clouds gathered overhead, and the premature chirping of crickets enveloped us in a high-pitched cocoon of sound.

I grinned as Natasha leaned back on two legs of her chair and reached for a candle and a box of matches on the counter behind her.

"I need a sorcerer who is also a kitsune. Or is that a kitsune who is a sorcerer?" I pressed my fingers to my forehead as a spike of pain stabbed through my skull. "Ugh. Thinking hurts. Got any magical pills for the pain?"

"You could have sent me a text you know?" She struck the match and the igniter spat sparks. The match-head flared to life and Natasha cupped it to protect the flame from the breeze flowing in through the open window.

"Huh?" I asked as she set the flame to the wick of the candle and watched the fire catch and the flame rise strong. "I didn't know you're now dial-a-sorcerer."

We both smiled, the movement more of a grimace than anything close to amusement. It was funny, but neither of us seemed to be in the mood for merriment.

I dug into the neckline of my shirt and lifted out the amulet she'd given me. "I'm not sure it works anymore."

She pursed her lips and reached out to hover her hand over the token, likely testing its energy. She shook her head. "It's still working. Something must be blocking the better part of its effectiveness. If it wasn't working at all, then it's likely you'd be dead by now."

I sighed. "That shouldn't be a problem. You'll just bring me right back."

She grinned. "So what do you need the kitsune for?"

I pulled my phone out of my pocket and swiped through my emails to find the images of the Chinese symbols Darius had given me. "These helped a great deal."

She pursed her lips, interested and impressed. "How do you know it works?"

I gave her a quick rundown of my stay in Hong Kong and the very satisfying absence of the poltergeist. I didn't say anything about Darius though, unsure if the ancient would approve. Here again I felt like a rotten friend.

I focused on answering her question. "It's these wards. They kept the *tokolosje* away while I was there. And I'm told that a kitsune sorcerer is the most ideal because they understand the ancient Eastern magic."

Natasha's pale head bobbed, sending her silken locks swaying around her shoulders. "Makes sense," she slid my phone back to me, "I'll find someone for you. I think I know of a guy in Mexico. But I have to check." She tilted her head and studied my face, her eyes watching me with such a knowing expression that I felt she could read into my soul.

And see me for the liar I am.

Sighing, I raised my glass—now encased in a layer of condensation—and slowly sipped more of my iced drink, trying to draw out the action.

Stalling.

And my guilt kicked in.

It cut deep into my gut, and like a knife left to sit within a raging fire, it left searing pain in its wake. I set the glass down carefully then pushed to my feet and tapped the table. "Since you've felt the need to hydrate me so well, I now need to pee."

Natasha's lips curved into an amused grin, her eyes sparkling with laughter. She wiggled her fingers at me—off you go.

I hurried down the hall to her bathroom. Her old-style farmhouse lacked the luxury of en-suite bathrooms and I was hoping I'd find what I was looking for in there.

And I did.

I'd expected it to be hard to obtain a strand of Natasha's hair, but given that she only allowed friends onto her property and that she'd erected a super powerful ward around the house, it wasn't likely that anyone could ever enter her home to rob her.

Probably why she didn't worry about leaving her hair lying around.

Because hair was one item that could be used against a person to perform all sorts of spells and curses, and it didn't matter if the magic was white or black, African or Eastern.

Pulling a Ziploc bag and a tweezer from my pocket—I seemed to have them always on my person these days—I slipped a strand of hair free from her hairbrush and deposited it safely within the confines of the plastic, which I tucked hurriedly back into my jeans pocket. Then I flushed the toilet, washed and dried my hands, and headed back to the kitchen.

Natasha was none the wiser.

And I felt like a piece of shit.

CHAPTER 18

I'd just reached the turnoff from Natasha's farmhouse onto the highway when my phone buzzed.

Steph sending me a text notifying me of the Phaser's *latest escapade* in Venice.

A branch of Garner diamonds had just been robbed.

Heading home, I parked outside our house, switched off the engine and locked the doors. I tossed the keys into the glovebox, grabbed my satchel and projected to the address Steph had sent.

Thankfully, the car, much like the truck, had very opaque tints so nobody would see me evaporating into thin air.

*V*enice was one of the European States, a collection of countries who'd long ago decided that being paranormal or displaying any form of special or unnatural power, meant instant death.

Long after the witch trials, the cities across the continent were still rife with minor factions and cults who made it their life's work to hunt down and kill people they suspected of being witches.

The saddest part was their sadistic effort rarely killed true paranormals. Instead, innocent human blood was spilled. One of the reasons supernaturals remained as much under the radar as possible while traveling through places like Venice or Milan or Amsterdam.

The cobbled streets were crowded, either with the dinner crowd or the mayhem caused by the robbery. Beautiful old buildings rose around me, ancient stone holding tales of the history they'd witnessed through hundreds of years.

On my right, the canal snaked away, a long slim gondola gliding across waters so still they appeared glassy.

A man on a bicycle whizzed past, almost brushing through my projected essence. The street was far too busy and I skimmed along to find a more private arrival location.

A block away, I found a darker alley, its narrow confines appeared safer than the bright city streets.

I jumped, regaining my balance as my feet hit solid ground. I checked the street and then hurried around the corner, heading up the street toward the commotion.

Blue fluorescent tape cordoned off an area outside the entrance of the store, a few uniformed gendarmeries posted outside, their faces molded into a sober seriousness that was more comical than frightening.

The post-robbery mayhem was visible through the storefront windows, the robbers having thrown jewelry and diamonds around in their rush to take what they wanted.

Seemed a very disorganized heist to me. Steph's message had said the police had claimed the Phaser had appeared to be helping, but we had another theory.

I texted Steph. "Get the CCTV feed."

"Already on it," she replied within seconds.

I smiled. I should have known. Steph was always one step ahead on the technical issues.

I shifted my gaze, and began to scan the crowd. One widely-known fact about crimes is perpetrators often returned to the scene to bask in the mayhem they caused. But, I wasn't entirely certain that the perpetrator wanted to cause mayhem for the general public.

What I did know was Elise Garner was holding out on me.

The crowd ebbed and flowed, some recording the scene for posterity or social media on their mobile phones, others merely standing and gossiping amongst themselves.

One man stood on the edge of the gathering, keeping a clear distance, which set him apart.

He wore jeans and a black leather hooded jacket, and his gray eyes were partially hidden by the dark glasses he wore. I only needed a second to project and verify that the onlooker was Erik Garner. He stood there for a few minutes, watching, his expression curious with a hint of gloating.

Then his gaze shifted toward me and he stiffened.

He turned away and hurried down the street, his swift gait revealing his need to get away as fast as possible. What had he seen about me that would make him flee? I began to follow him, turning in his direction quickly to keep up.

Someone shoved me aside really hard, as he hurried through the throng.

In Erik's direction.

So he hadn't seen *me*. Our vigilante had a stalker.

I followed the man as he followed Erik, waiting only until I was clear of witnesses. Erik led the man deeper into the warren of alleyways that often narrowed so much that a person could barely fit in the slim space.

Erik was halfway down the long alley with his stalker at his back, when he stopped in his tracks. Beyond him another man, long black coat and hat matching Erik's stalker, stood staring at him.

Crap.

There were two of them.

I tugged a black hoodie from my satchel and drew it on, pulling the hood low over my face. Then I jumped, grabbed a hold of Erik and jumped him a few blocks away. He landed startled, then struck out at me wildly.

Disoriented, he slammed against the wall behind him staring at me in terror.

For all his age and his vigilante antics he was still a young boy. "Don't be afraid."

Even as I spoke, he began to phase through the wall, the form of his body becoming intangible as he sank into the brickwork.

I held out a hand. "Wait. I saved your life, the least you could do is talk to me for a few seconds."

He returned his body to the street and became solid again, watching me warily. "What do you want?"

I kept my distance and leaned against the wall behind me, folding my arms. "I'm Mel. I'm a jumper."

"No shit," he sneered, then pointed at his eyes. "See these? They're called eyes. And they work fine."

I grinned. "Look. I'm not here to apprehend you. I just wanted to talk."

"What about?"

"Your mother." He stiffened, then began to phase again. "Don't you want to know why I haven't already taken you back to her?"

He stopped and stared at me, not saying a word.

"And don't waste your time running from me. I can find you wherever you go, and I can stop you even if you're phasing."

A total lie, but I spoke them with a straight face.

CHAPTER 19

His eyes darkened at my words and he began to phase.

I folded my arms and watched, my expression nonchalant, my nerves shot. The last thing I wanted to do was to lose him, and I prayed my play would work.

Something in my demeanor must have convinced him because he stopped vibrating, became solid and said, "I don't believe you can stop me mid-phase, but I'll give you the benefit of the doubt."

I shook my head and straightened from the wall.

"What do you want?" he fidgeted with the ties of his hood, "Why haven't you taken me yet?"

"Because too many of the pieces in this case are falling in all the wrong places."

He gave a hesitant nod. "But she's paying you."

I shrugged. "I'm not concerned about the money. And a verbal contract given under a false guise, is null and void."

He smiled. "You don't trust her, do you?"

I shook my head. "She said all the right things. But a few of those things don't add up."

He inhaled. "Okay. I'll talk to you, but not here."

He was already walking off, leaving me to hurry in his wake. I didn't ask questions, just strode along a few feet behind him so an observer wouldn't assume we were together.

A few blocks later, he made a sharp left into a narrow alley, went up a short flight of stone steps then another ten yards later he slowed to a stop.

I glanced behind me and found the street empty. Up ahead the situation was the same.

Erik lifted a foot and touch the toe of his boot to a brick low on the wall. Seeing through glamors had always been an advantage and I could make out the glyph etched into the stone. It glowed red and yellow, marking the place as a safe haven for paranormals.

"I wasn't aware Venice had any of these," I murmured as he phased. I jumped following him inside to land in a dank and darkened hallway. A second ward of glamor made the hall look old, with rotting walls and water-stains on ragged moldy carpet.

Beyond the haze of the glamor was a door, and from the inner room came the low clamor of laughter and the thrum of music.

Erik led me past the glamor and opened the door, beckoning me to enter with the most perfect manners. Then, he waved a hand at the corner table along the front wall, hidden in shadows and within easy access to a swift departure. Should someone enter and scan the place, we wouldn't be seen immediately.

We sat and he waved a hand at the bartender who began to pour without even asking. I frowned but figured it didn't matter. I wasn't here to drink anyway.

I leaned forward, met the boy's eyes and said, "So, why does your mother want me to find you?"

He lifted his chin "Because I know her secret."

"Which is?"

He looked away. "I'd prefer not to put you in any danger."

I leaned back and chuckled. "I'm always in danger. What's one more lot of danger added to the mix." He looked back at me.

"Look, your mother asked me to investigate. I can't be held responsible for what I discover."

He gave a short nod, but he met my eyes only for a few short seconds and then studied the wrought iron chandelier above our heads as if the candles, with their magical yellow flames and fake dripping wax, were far more interesting than the problem of his over-possessive mother.

I leaned forward and said, "She wants me to bring you in. Give me a reason not to."

I hadn't felt any reason to take the kid in. Until now, he hadn't done anything wrong. Technically, he owned the stores he was robbing.

Hold on a second.

"You aren't taking from the stores are you?"

He squinted at me, his expression tense.

Aware.

I smiled. "You're roughing the places up, making it look like a robbery but you're not taking anything."

He grinned back. "How did you figure it out?" His grin made him look young again, a little less haunted.

"I just don't picture you as a thief. And I'm guessing these *robberies* are a way to warn your mother."

He nodded, then stopped speaking as the bartender arrived with our drinks. A strawberry milkshake for the vigilante, and a glass of sparkling water for me. I stared at the man, confused.

"What did I get?" I asked, looking longingly at the milkshake.

He smiled, flashing a gold tooth. "You got exactly what you wanted."

I raised an eyebrow. What I'd wanted was a glass of fae beer. Something that I hadn't drunk in almost a year. He nodded at the glass.

I lifted it and sipped carefully, my eyes widening as the delicious sweetness hit my tongue.

"Where in the world did you get fae beer?"

He raised his eyebrows and tucked his thumbs into his belt loops. "If I tell ya, I'll have to kill ya."

I snorted.

He tapped his forefinger to his temple in an abbreviated salute and headed back to the bar.

"He's got connections across all the planes. It's how he manages to obtain so many different types of drinks."

I nodded at his milkshake. "You went for the mundane."

He shook his head. "Nope. This is an elvin plum milkshake. I bet you thought it was strawberry."

I laughed softly. "Okay, you got me."

He sipped then said, "My mother has a secret so bad that the Supreme High Council would haul her ass to jail on a life sentence if they found out."

"Oh," I said softly. It didn't surprise me. The woman was far too calculating to have been a merely worried mother. "So she's trying to stop you from revealing the truth?"

He nodded. "I stayed away from her since I left home. I thought I'd be able to put her and my old life behind me."

"What happened?"

He sighed and sat back, staring off into the distance. "My trust fund kicked in on my eighteenth birthday and my bank account was suddenly overflowing with zeros."

"She didn't stop the transfer?" He shook his head. "And you think she's trying to buy your silence?" I murmured.

"She sure as hell is. But it won't work. I will bring her to justice. But I need to be smart about it."

I leaned closer. "How can I help?"

He gave me a narrow-eyed stare. "This isn't some game. It's dangerous."

"You think I don't know that?" His face was expressionless. I reached across the table and offered him my hand. "Hi. My name is Mel Morgan."

He blanched, staring at my hand and then at my face. "The SoulTracker?"

"The one and only."

He shifted in his seat. "I'm sorry. I had no idea."

I lifted a shoulder. "It's cool. Not everyone knows me by sight. I tend to move under the radar as much as possible."

"But your reputation precedes you."

I made a face. "So. Tell me what's going on with your mother and we'll figure it out. I have contacts at the Supreme High Council, as well as Sentinel. I can protect you if that's what you need. And I can help you bring her to justice if that's what she deserves."

He nodded, drained his drink and inhaled. "When I was fifteen I played hooky in Hong Kong, and went to visit my mother at her office. She hadn't expected me to walk into her office in the middle of the day. I sometimes wonder why she'd been so careless.

"When I entered her office, the place was empty but I heard sounds as if it came from an adjoining room. I discovered a bookshelf that was slightly misaligned and opened it to find a small room behind it. She'd had her back to me and was talking to a man, bound to a metal chair with chains.

"At first, I'd thought it was something kinky, but she was demanding that he increase production. He told her he could only do so much so fast. If she wanted to push him and he died in the process then it was her loss.

"She laughed and said that there were more of him. And that apparently his daughter was just as talented."

Erik shook his head and looked away. "She laughed at him . . ." he said softly, "her tone was so cold, so unfeeling and cruel, I could hardly believe she was my mother."

He began to fidget, scraping the soft wood of the table with his fingernail. I wanted to do something—pat his hand or his arm —but I got the feeling that if I did he'd clam up on me. So I held my breath and hoped he'd spill everything without chickening out.

Erik shifted in his seat, sitting up straighter. He met my gaze, and the sadness and self-recrimination were so clear in his eyes. "I never would have thought she'd do something this horrible, but I'm beginning to wonder if this is who she truly is and that I've been naive and blind to it all my life." He paused, the cleared his throat. "Do you know what an Agamas Elf is?"

I nodded. "Very rare elf whose fingers emit lightning on command. Mythically known to create diamonds. *If* they are extremely talented."

I paused, my mouth open.

"Oh."

It fell into place within a second. Elise Garner was holding an Agamas Elf prisoner and threatening his family to ensure he continued to make diamonds for her.

"This is a whole new level of 'blood diamond'."

$\mathcal{E}$rik nodded, his skin now looking gray from the tension. "Rumpelstiltskin gone bad."

"You can say that again."

We sat there in silence for a few minutes.

What in the world was my next step?

"We need to stop her." Erik slammed a fist onto the table. "And however we do it, we have to ensure that the elf's family is removed from danger."

Erik was quiet as he spun his empty glass in place.

"You have a plan."

He shrugged. "The most I'd hoped for was to cause mayhem to her business. Make people feel like Garner diamonds were a risk."

I rubbed my forehead. I felt a headache coming. Last thing I needed, not when I had so much going on. "We need to ensure she's caught in the act."

"How do we do that?"

"It would be easy enough to enter the hidden room and retrieve the elf, but we need evidence if we want the Supreme

High Council to arrest her and hold her accountable for her crimes."

"So? We put a camera in the room?"

I nodded. He was definitely a smart kid. "I will project first. See if the place is clear. Then I'll jump through and install the camera."

"You can't go alone."

I frowned. "Why not?"

"What if she's got the place rigged to trap paranormals?"

"Not much can hold a teleporter."

"She pays a lot for dark magic wards." He looked worried.

I studied his face. "Then? What do you suggest?"

"Let me go." I suspected that he'd offer himself up.

I shook my head. "No way. Chances are she'll trap you there. She paid me to find you. I doubt you'll be allowed to enter the place and then just leave because you feel like it."

He smiled slowly. "I can phase through anything. That's what makes her uneasy. Nothing stops me." I lifted an eyebrow. "I'm not bragging. It's a scientific fact. I can vibrate my body to such an extent that I can even pass through lead. I've done the testing."

"So even dark magic won't hold you?"

He shook his head. "I'm not sure why. If I try really hard I can get through a magical ward. It knocks the shit out of me, but I can do it."

I sighed. "Okay. If you're sure."

He smiled, a light sparking in his eyes. "I've broken into banks in Geneva. I think I can handle my mother's office."

"Don't get cocky. If she's been keeping the elf hostage all this while, what makes you think she wouldn't have the place guarded. She could have cameras watching the entrance to the room."

He pursed his lips as he considered my words. "I'm thinking I'll come in through the outer wall. She's leasing an entire floor. Corner office, But the secret room had no windows. It's probably boarded up. Could be concrete, or a wood panel, I'm not sure. Either way it doesn't matter because I can phase through it."

"You just need to get outside the building." I folded my arms. "How many floors up is that?" I smirked.

He nodded, flushing. "Okay. Bad plan. Unless you know someone who can fly me up there."

I sighed and leaned closer. "Look. The best way to do this is a two-pronged attack. We go together. I'll meet with her. While I'm talking to her, she'll be distracted. How about you phase into the elevator shaft, get a ride up on the outside of the elevator and wait there for me." He nodded slowly. "As soon as I get into her office you phase into the room and set up the camera."

"The elf might not let you do it, though."

"Why the heck not?" he scowled. He wasn't enjoying the holes I was shooting in his plans.

"Because he may feel his actions would put his daughter in graver danger."

"Oh."

"So let me do a quick recon. I have a feeling they'll be keeping her somewhere in the building."

In fact, I wouldn't put it past Elise Garner to have both father and daughter in captivity and play the two off each other using the threat of injury to keep them producing her diamonds.

Erik tilted his head and stared at me as he put two-and-two together. "You think she's holding the both of them in the building?"

Mind-reader much. "I do."

He laughed. "I guess you know my mother even better than I do."

"It's not that. It's merely because as her child you'd want to hold onto some kind of hope that your mother is innocent."

Erik nodded and leaned his elbows on the table. He brushed his fingers through his dark hair, ruffling it up until it stuck out in all directions. His frustration showed in the shadows beneath his eyes, and the stiff way he held his shoulders. I felt impotent, unable to do much more to free him from his mother's chains.

Then he inhaled harshly and gave the table a small thump with his fist. He met my eyes. "So when do we do this?"

"I guess there's no time like the present?" I sat back and studied him, "the Venice store is in shambles. Do you think your mother would come to inspect it in person?"

Erik shook his head. "I don't think so. She'd probably want to look at the video footage. And more than likely she'd send one of her assistants to check the problem out. Damage control. Stock management et cetera."

"So she's not going to come running when one of her stores has been robbed?" I found that hard to believe.

"I can't see her doing that unless she's absolutely sure they took something."

I lifted a brow and smiled. "So *did* they take something?"

He nodded, giving me a toothy grin. "Of course, they took something. What do you think the whole charade was for?"

Erik shook his head and fiddled in the pocket of his hoodie. He withdrew a large pink diamond, which glistened in the palm of his hand as it caught the flickering candlelight from above.

"This is what I took. But I didn't make it easy for her to find out. I left a fake in its place . . . a very good fake that would take time for her to figure it out."

"Why this particular diamond?" I reached for the beautiful stone.

Erik dropped it in my palm and watched as I twirled it between my fingers. "Because this is not an elf-made stone. This is a true blood diamond."

My eyes widened in shock and I dropped the stone to the table instinctively. I'd always hated the idea of the blood-diamond trade. I'd known a few people in my time who'd been extremely happy to flaunt a giant-sized stone on their ring-finger without giving a single thought to how that jewel had been procured, how much blood had been spilled in the effort to obtain it.

Erik scooped the diamond up and put it back into his pocket.

I swallowed hard and slowly withdrew my hand from the surface of the table. I scrubbed my palm against the fabric of my jeans, as if the mere action would wipe away the remnants of my contact with the jewel. I knew it would do nothing to help the way I felt, but I did it anyway.

Erik smiled, almost as if he could see my hand through the table. "This is *the* most expensive, *the* most rare item in the Venice store. Mother likes to spread the most exclusive stones around the world. This particular pink diamond is so extremely rare that there is none other like it. Something about the color and the facets, and of course its size. It's the kind of jewel Kings and Queens would buy."

I nodded. I'd begun to understand the way Erik Garner thought. And I had to admit taking the diamond had been a smart move. "So what happens when she discovers that it's gone?"

He smiled. "She'll go ballistic."

"Would she suspect you?"

He shrugged. "She might. But I don't care." Erik's youth and naiveté were clear. He obviously didn't understand the ramifications.

"If she suspects you, then she'll have increased her security to keep an eye out for you."

Erik shook his head. "She's so afraid of me only because she can't stop me from going where I want, when I want. She's tried for years to do that, tried and failed. It frustrates her that she can't stop me, no matter how hard she tries."

I sat back and stared at the boy. "So your mother has been unable to find a way to prevent you from seeing things that could jeopardize her position and reputation."

He nodded.

I tapped the top of the table with my nail. "This might be a problem if I decide to walk into her office now. If she knows you were here at the Venice robbery—and she would by now—she'd think I'm completely incompetent because I didn't catch you."

Erik wriggled in his seat. "It doesn't really matter. Let's get moving and put the plan in motion."

"It does matter," I leaned closer, "As soon as she gets word that the diamond is missing, she'll know it was you. I would rather not have her guarded. What I *would* like is for her to be off-balance and confused when she finds that nothing is missing. "

"You want me to return the diamond?" Erik asked reluctantly.

I nodded. "I know what you want to achieve, but unfortunately . . . right now . . . for the plan to succeed we can't have her on guard. She will be frustrated enough after the robbery."

Erik sighed and gave a reluctant nod. "Fine. I'll return it."

I shook my head. "I have a better plan."

He quirked an eyebrow.

"Give it to me," I smiled at his surprise, "I don't have a Plan B. So we need Plan A to sweep her off her feet before she even realizes what's happening."

Erik's jaw dropped as he stared at me, stunned. "You're going to just give it back to her?"

"Yup. I'm going to stun her with a major coup, then question the origins of the stone."

He grinned. "That'll do it. She'll pave your way in gold if she thought it would stop you from talking." Then he paused. "That, or she'll have you killed."

I snorted. "Don't worry. She'd have to stand in line and from the looks of it she'd be too late anyway."

"What?" asked Erik, straightening with surprise.

"Long story," I waved him off as I got to my feet. "Are you going to provide the camera?"

He nodded. "Don't worry. I have that sorted. How soon do we leave?"

"We leave Venice tonight. Our only problem is I have no way of explaining to Elise how I got from Venice to Hong Kong within hours of the robbery."

Erik made a rude sound. "Yeah. Flight time's thirteen hours at the least."

As much as the time zones annoyed me, it wasn't something we could control.

"You get the camera. I'll wait here for you. We can go to Chicago and wait it out there."

Erik nodded and left the bar, leaving me to survey the patrons. A room full of supernaturals was a rare sight, glamors all fighting against each other to hide the truth of what they are. Even O'Hagan's was never this packed to the brim.

I headed over to the bar where the bartender was industriously shining glasses and wiping off the already spotless surface of his mahogany bar.

"What can I do for you?"

"What's on the menu?" A sudden growl emanated from my stomach. Great. My stomach can perform on cue now, like a circus animal.

He gave me a smile, "No menu."

I nodded really slowly. "Ookay." I stopped my eyes from rolling and returned to my table, disappointed and more hungry than ever.

I pulled my phone from my jacket pocket and texted Steph.

Anything?

She responded within seconds.

Cameras are malfunctioning. Nothing to show.

I wasn't surprised.

Heard from Drake?

I got a no.

Saleem came by looking for you. He's . . . antagonized.

Stall.

I felt bad to ask her to be the intermediary but Saleem

wouldn't be happy to know I was jumping, let alone on a dangerous case. Now that he knew what I was up against he'd turn into the overprotective boyfriend.

While I waited for Erik, I did a quick projection and tried to see if I could find some kind of track that would lead me to Samuel again.

I drew a blank.

Despondent now, I slid my phone back into my pocket, the sound of plastic crinkling beneath my fingers. I'd totally forgotten about the samples that I was supposed to be gathering.

So, while I waited for Erik—I slid further into the shadows and projected to the Murdochs' apartment.

Thankfully it was empty and I navigated my way toward the captain's bedroom, in search of a hairbrush. Unfortunately, I came up empty. But I did manage to discover a razor on the sink.

I jumped straight into his bathroom, grabbed the razor and returned to the bar in Venice before quickly depositing it into another plastic bag. Samuel, the Murdochs, Steph, Saleem, Natasha and Drake; all ticked off my list. I now had Storm left.

Possibly Kailin?

I wasn't sure about that but I figured if I was going to betray those closest to me, I may as well go the whole hog and alienate everyone I cared about.

Never let it be said that Mel Morgan did anything by halves.

The samples I already had should be plenty to go on, so I sent a quick text to a certain kitsune I knew, and asked him for a drop-off location.

He responded almost immediately, happy to be of service, asking me to come to his suite—the address of my most recent bout as his captive.

After a quick projection to make sure the coast was clear, I gathered all the bags, made the jump to Hong Kong, and arrived in front of Darius's exuberant assistant.

Not in the mood to waste time, I handed over the packets

which I'd labeled with each owner's name, and left without saying a word.

I returned to the table just in time, as the barkeep was already heading toward me, bearing a tray of food.

I tried not to look surprised when he set a bowl of *jalevi* in front of me. The dish was exquisite, something I'd come across once when I'd projected to the Dragon realm. Made from the meat of a cow-like animal, it was technically a beef paella, with the succulent, falling-off-the-bone beef comprising the meat of the dish.

I flashed the barkeep a grateful smile, but refrained from asking him how he'd procured the meal this time.

He had to be a gnome. They were known to travel far and wide in order to procure an item, and usually charged extortionist fees.

What would this meat cost me? I tried to put it out of my mind and concentrated on my food

Only when I'd downed the first delicious bite did I realize how ravenous I was. The lilting music around me was comforting, and the rumble of laughter and conversation enveloped me in its warmth.

I'd just finished my meal when Erik arrived, a triumphant smile on his face. He set a black bag on the table. "Camera obtained, as you requested."

I wiped my mouth with a paper towel and dropped it into the empty bowl. "Right. I'm ready to leave as soon as you are." I glanced at my watch. "Time now in Hong Kong? Will your mother be awake if it's too late?"

"The woman doesn't know what sleep is."

I shrugged. "I just wondered if she needed her beauty sleep," I hid my smile as I bagged the camera and got to my feet, "Let's pay and get moving."

Erik waved a hand at me. "It's okay. I put it on my tab. Besides, I owe you considering you didn't take me straight to

Mother dearest." Then he paused. "Wait a second. You're not taking me straight to my mother."

He looked disappointed.

Despite Erik's dissatisfaction with my plan, he had no choice. And neither did I.

We had to assume that Elise knew nothing about the supernatural world. And if she was ignorant of it the last thing we needed was to make her curious.

"I'll call her now. Make an appointment to see her. Let's just hope she doesn't tell me she's booked solid for the week."

Despite my words, I had a good feeling Elise Garner would not turn me away. I'd seen a certain desperation in her eyes, and I knew the woman wanted her son found. I had to admit that she scared me a little. She'd displayed an icy ruthlessness, even when it was directed at her own flesh and blood.

I made a mental note to check with Storm, because I was beginning to suspect that Elise Garner was a mage of some sort. Nothing outwardly obvious, even to a paranormal like me, but something nonetheless.

Placing the call, I was surprised when Elise herself answered considering it was still the early hours of the morning in Hong Kong. I'd expected to leave a message.

She seemed equally surprised to hear from me, her strained voice confirmed she was distracted. She agreed to meet at 5pm her evening at her office.

Her tone had been clear; don't be late.

When I rang off from my call with Elise, Erik's expression was withdrawn as he stared at his phone.

"What's up?" I asked, worried that he may be changing his mind.

He glanced at me. "I won't come with you to Chicago. There's something I need to do first. I'll meet you here at 3pm Hong Kong time?"

I hesitated, wanting to say no, but I couldn't control his movements. And any attempt to restrict him could backfire too.

My phone buzzed, announcing an incoming text.

Package from Fulbright in your study.

Saleem had come through. Not that I'd doubted him for a second.

I focused on Erik and gave him a neutral smile, then held my palm open. I had only one piece of collateral that I could ask for to ensure he didn't just disappear and leave me to deal with his mother alone.

Erik gave a rueful smile and withdrew the diamond as well as a small velvet-covered case. He flipped it open and placed the stone on a bed of white silk.

Closing the case, he handed it over to me with a smile, gave me his cell phone number and then phased away through the wall.

Guy made an impressive exit.

A second buzzing from my phone had me checking the screen again. Force of habit, or just eager to communicate with Saleem?

Spoke to Logan. He's agreed to join my team and go to the Mithras with me. He's offered extra firepower. A couple more bodies too, just in case.

He sounded a little more enthusiastic and I smiled to myself, glad that Logan's inclusion into the mission had eased Saleem's pre-mission planning stress.

I'd never felt comfortable with Saleem keeping the truth from Logan, but I'd never pretended to understand the way the male mind worked.

I was just glad that Logan, with his power and his experience, would have Saleem's back during the mission, and whatever the djinn world had waiting.

The only thing that surprised me was how fast Saleem and Logan were moving on this. He'd said 'just recon' but who knew what that meant.

My fingers curled around the phone and I inhaled slowly.

Given that Saleem had progressed from I-should-maybe-make-a-plan to we're-about-to-head-out, I figured it was time to give Saleem's mom a head's up.

I teleported to my study and caught sight of the small envelope sitting in the center of the desk.

Dropping my satchel on the desk, I grabbed the envelope and headed upstairs. Inhaling slowly, I listened to the house. The place was silent except for the hum of the old refrigerator and the energy emanating from the ward around the house and the comms room upstairs.

No sign of the poltergeist.

Not yet, anyway.

I shrugged off my negativity and crossed my fingers as I headed down the hall to my bedroom.

I sat on the bed, ripping open Saleem's envelope and was surprised when two sets of samples came tumbling onto my lap.

The first bore a white rectangular label with Fulbright's name scrawled in black ink. I studied the two strands of oily brown hair and sent Saleem my virtual gratitude.

The second bag made me go cold.

The clear plastic revealed two long strands of black hair. The label said *Saleem.*

I took a deep breath, stowed the samples inside the hidey-hole and wandered downstairs, my mind on Saleem.

Sinking onto the sofa, I sent a quick text to Steph, giving her an update on the djinn mission in progress, fake robberies in Venice, Agamas elves in captivity and pink blood diamonds.

Then dropped my phone at my side and lay back against the pillows, fatigue getting the best of me.

Saleem had felt the need to clear himself from my suspect list, volunteering his DNA for testing. That he'd done so made me wonder how he felt about being on the list at all.

Was he upset? Or angry? I wouldn't blame him either way.

Sucking in a harsh breath, I pushed the thoughts away and closed my eyes.

I had a quick visit to make to a certain queen.

~

I closed my eyes and projected into the ether, using the Djinn Queen's feedback thread to guide me straight to her.

The mansion in which Omega was keeping her was well warded, but safe. Even Saleem had grown used to the idea of his mother remaining in captivity until they found a smarter and safer way to extract her.

She was comfortable enough with her own large suite, and vintage furnishings, a stark contrast to a cold, bare cell.

I transitioned from the ether, and slid through the gap in the Veil, lowering my essence into her room. I got my bearings inside the large living area, finding her standing beside the gigantic window, staring out onto the grounds.

Queen Aisha's profile was regal—back straight, chin slightly jutting out—her bearing even more so. The woman was not one to be messed with.

She wore a long green silk kaftan-style dress and from the basket filled with colored threads and needles on the table behind her, I expected the intricate embroidery to be her creation.

Impressed, I skittered forward without hesitation, not stopping even when her spine stiffened, telling me she knew I was there. She was intimidating, but I liked her.

And she didn't scare me.

"I wonder if that's a good thing," she murmured as I drew to a halt beside her.

Cringing, I remembered too late that she could read my mind. Regaining my composure, I said, "Why would it not be a good thing? It's not as if we're about to head off on a girl's spa day."

My comment brought a smile to her face, one which she kept directed on the view. The large multi-paned window reached to within a foot from the high ceiling. A wide cushioned seat filled the bottom of the window, but the queen remained on her feet, her spine straight, her eyes on the wide expanse of green that was the back lawn of the property.

The old French-styled manor house had held the queen captive within its walls for more than a year now and the only thing good about it was she'd been kept in relative comfort.

"Nice needlework," I whispered.

"Are you being facetious?" Amusement warred with annoyance in her tone.

I smiled, even though I knew she couldn't see me. "The plan is a go."

"Saleem has left for Mithras, then." She sighed and straightened her dress, the green silk rustling as she moved. "I pray that he is in time."

I wasn't sure what to say. Praying wouldn't change what was going to happen, whether it was fate—or us—who controlled our destiny, every action we performed had a result.

And that combination of action and result would be difficult to be directed by a simple prayer.

"You are very pragmatic, my dear."

I made a sound in my head that I knew she wouldn't hear; one of frustration because she always lulled me into feeling at ease, so much so that I often forgot she could read my thoughts.

"I thought you should know that he's left."

The queen gave an almost imperceptible nod, one only I could see and understand. "It's considerate of you to come."

I gave an ethereal shrug. "Not like I could call your cell or anything."

She snorted, the sound oddly regal.

Letting out a sigh, I said, "I'd better get going. There's a lot happening right now." I found myself strangely sad to leave. And more puzzled by it than ever.

She nodded, the light playing on her features, the shadowed hollows of her eyes making her look almost skeletal. I studied her again, wondering at the toll her incarceration would have taken on her.

I cleared my throat. "I'm waiting until I hear back from them. As soon as Saleem tells me they're safe and things are under control, I'll be back here to get you to safety."

Her lips tightened into a thin smile but her eyes sparkled. She was controlling the urge to laugh.

"Okay, fine," I controlled the urge to sigh, "I'll let you know so *you* can get yourself to safety."

I rolled my eyes.

Then stiffened. Hopefully she hadn't seen that

When she snorted just as I left the room, I knew she had.

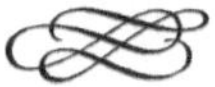

My phone was buzzing when I returned to my body, Kailin Odel's name blinking bright green. I slid my finger across the screen, expecting the familiar voice on the other end.

My smiling greeting faded away as soon as I heard the desperation and fear in Kai's voice.

"Mel?" she asked, her voice shaking.

"Kailin? What's wrong?" my voice rose as I spoke, spurred by the fear almost tangible through the phone.

"I can't . . ." She took a breath and cleared her throat. "I need help finding Anjelo. He's in trouble. I'm at Storm's place."

"Where's Storm. Can he not help?" I asked, more worried now.

Kai made an odd sound in her throat. "Storm's not who we thought he was."

I frowned, and was about to ask her to explain when she cut me off.

"Please Mel. It's urgent. My friend Anjelo . . . his life is in danger. Can you come now?"

She didn't need to repeat the question. Kailin Odel, Alpha of the Panther Walker clan, was my friend. And I'd never heard her sound this afraid before, even when she'd asked for my help in saving her mother.

And whatever she was saying about Storm—while I didn't believe it for a minute—I could clarify it with her later.

"Give me two minutes." I rang off without waiting for her response. Tucking my phone into my jacket pocket, I hurried to the study, grabbed my satchel and checked for my dagger and weapons.

Heading to the kitchen, I grabbed a sheet of paper from the notepad on the kitchen counter and scratched out a quick note to Steph.

Leaving the note on the kitchen table I projected to Kai, tracking her through the ether using her familiar feedback threads. All clear, I straightened my shoulders, shoving down my fatigue as far as I could, and jumped straight to her.

The jump wore me out, but thankfully I didn't have a bloody nose episode. I could deal with being tired.

I materialized and tucked my hair behind my ears as I arrived. Standing in front of the elevators in Storm's apartment building, Kailin stared at me, her normally bright green eyes huge, and dull.

And stricken.

"Are you okay?" she asked softly.

I gave her a quick nod, and forced a smile on my face. I was more concerned with the panic I saw in her eyes than my own issues. "I'm fine. Just a whole lot going on."

"Is Saleem okay?" Kai asked, stepping closer. "He hasn't been answering our calls and I'm starting to worry." Her eyes were enough to confirm her concern.

Shaking my head, I tugged the strap of my satchel higher up my shoulder. "He's okay," I studied Kai's face, trying to understand why she was evading the real reason she'd called me here, "he had to go home to see his brother."

Her eyes widened. "Home as in Djinn-world home?" She looked a little stunned.

I nodded, trying not to show how much his absence worried me, how hard it was for me to not be with him on this journey that he was taking to his home . . . to danger unknown. More especially, I wondered if my guilt was written all over my face.

Kai studied my face, and looked as if she was about to drill me, but then her expression shifted. Without a word she held out her hand and beckoned me to follow her upstairs to Storm's apartment.

I followed and soon we stood in front of his door. Kai stared at the locked door. Made of steel and inches thick, it was almost impenetrable.

"It's made of steel," said Lily.

I glanced at the lynx walker. Her eyes were red and shimmering with tears. She and Anjelo were a couple, inseparable as far as I knew. And both of them were as close to Kailin as siblings.

If anything happened to Anjelo, I suspected Lily wasn't the only one who'd suffer the loss.

I swallowed hard and nodded. "I'll check first." I shut my eyes for a few seconds, projecting inside the room. Satisfied the place was empty, I opened my eyes and gave the scared girl an encouraging smile. Her eyes were round, her shoulders set in an I'm-taking-no-crap stance.

"All clear," I said, "see you soon."

I jumped straight into the room and began to open the half dozen locks securing the door. Strange that Storm felt the need to lock himself away like that. Being an Immortal, I was sure he'd have more powers than that of your average man.

I opened the door, and Kai paused. Lily hovered on the threshold, her fear emphasized by the dark circles under her eyes.

Why was she so afraid?

I frowned and glanced at Kai, wondering what the heck was going on here? But the fear in my friend's eyes was tangible and I had to accept that as much as I was in the dark, she'd explain it all soon enough.

Kai entered and walked past me, doing a quick one-eighty of the living room. Finding it empty she rushed deeper into the apartment, searching in vain. I could have told her the place was empty, and I suspected she knew as much. But she moved out of instinct, out of basic need.

Her search came up empty and she returned to the hallway, watching Lily, her eyes concerned but determined. "Can you think where they would have taken him? Was there someplace else that you heard him mention?"

Lily frowned. Her golden lynx eyes shifting to a deep molasses, her energy telling me she was aching to explode.

"If you can't manage it, then don't push yourself too hard, okay?" Kai said softly, tipping her head close to meet the younger girl's eyes.

When Lily finally spoke, her words sent a chill through me. "I do remember Storm mentioning something about sending kids away to a special facility. I think they had something special planned for Logan."

Logan? What happened to Logan?

I stared at Kai, desperate to know more but understanding too how fragile Lily was. So I held my curiosity at bay and paid attention as Lily's forehead furrowed. "I wish I could remember more. All I know is that Storm would email the people at some facility to keep them updated on Logan's whereabouts."

What the heck?

"Did he actually talk about this in front of you?" Kai asked, her eyes wide with disbelief. She didn't seem at all surprised at Lily's accusation and she looked unimpressed that Storm would discuss such details with Lily as a witness.

What was Kai thinking?

I knew what I'd be wondering. If Storm was this bad guy they were making him out to be, then I'd need to think of him as a bad guy. And bad guys never talk about sensitive stuff in front of captives unless said captive was about to meet with a dead end.

Lily's head bobbed up and down. "Yes. It's like he wanted me to know everything he was doing. Like it was a game. Sometimes he'd keep me tied up in the front room, facing all the monitors on the wall so that I could see what was happening."

Was Storm the same person Lily was talking about? This couldn't be true.

"Monitors," Kai asked.

"Yes." Lily whispered with a nod as she turned and walked over to the wall on the left and searched the top of the mantelpiece.

After a few seconds she retrieved a remote control, pressed a button and aimed it at the wall.

The wall shifted and a panel slid up, revealing a series of monitors, all showing videos of various locations and people. From the digital clocks on the corners of each monitor it was clear the feeds were live.

One of the screens showed a pretty young redhead, walking in a park.

I glanced over at Kai and stopped in my tracks. The terrified look on her face confirmed she'd seen something, the tears in her eyes said it was bad.

I tracked her gaze to a monitor that showed camera feed from a hospital room where Anjelo lay, unmoving, tubes leaving and entering his body in a convoluted mess.

My heart tightened as I watched Kai protect Lily from the sight, moving so Lily would look at her and not at the monitor. Watched as Kai blinked away tears and tried to remain strong.

I hurried over to Kai. "What do you need me to do?"

She glanced up at my face. We'd been through a fair amount of drama together, and despite my worry, and my concern about how Storm was entangled in this mess, helping Kai when she needed me was my top priority.

"Just hold on for two seconds while I send a text."

She cocked her chin at Lily and I nodded, heading over to the girl. Holding her around her shoulders, I guided her to the sofa and sat her down so she faced the floor-to-ceiling windows. I'd been in this room not so long ago and I'd had no idea what was going on behind walls and hidden in rooms.

What was Storm doing? And why?

Glancing over at Kai, I wondered who she was texting. Her expression was an odd blend of annoyance and relief so I hoped she was making progress.

As she tapped her foot and waited, she glanced up at the screen, her spine stiffening so sharply that I had to look for myself.

The screen showed Anjelo, tied to a metal table, a couple of orderlies hovering around him, untying the straps around his ankles and wrists. They piled him onto a gurney and disappeared off-screen. Panic filled Kai's eyes and I rubbed Lily's back hoping she wouldn't choose that moment to turn around.

Kai's cellphone bleeped and then she was tapping messages and her foot in turn.

A few seconds later she waved at me and met my gaze, relief and hope shining in her green eyes. "I know where he is."

I rose and Lily followed suit, the two of us hurrying to Kai, eager to get on with it.

"Let's get going then," I said, looking pointedly at the monitors and then sending Kai a questioning glance. Kai chose to ignore it and proceeded to send off another barrage of texts.

Finally she gave me a nod. "We need to get to Omega. They're keeping Logan in a facility within the building. Daniel couldn't be any more specific than that, so we'll have to do some searching."

I wasn't listening to anything else.

Logan?

Logan was being kept in an Omega facility. Which meant he wasn't with Saleem. Which meant either Saleem lied to me about Logan joining him on his Mithras mission, or something had happened to change their plans.

I was hoping the latter.

I hid my confusion and nodded, not bothering to ask who Daniel was. "You two wait here. I'll do a quick recon." I projected, following Logan's feedback, tracking it back from the last contact he'd made with Kailin.

I saw the room, as if in a nightmare, all cold and lifeless. And Logan, encased in a metal pod, covered by a swirling white vapor and crystals of ice.

Sucking in a harsh breath, my eyes snapped open.

"Come," I said, my voice a little shaky, "I found him."

Lily and Kai each took a hold of one of my hands, and I jumped. We arrived inside the shadowed room, right beside a closed metal door. A light shone from the room beyond it, and my heart stuttered, worried more now for Kai and how she was going to take Logan's condition.

Kai looked a little unsettled, yet still determined.

"Where are we?" Lily whispered, her lynx eyes taking on an eerie glow as she probed the darkness with her night vision.

"We're in the room next to the one where they're keeping Logan. See, over there," I spoke softly, pointing at the window beside me. It revealed another room right next door.

Kai's horrified gasp sliced deep into me, and I felt her pain, knew how I'd feel if one of my own loved ones were in a similar position.

Her words were whispered, and yet in my ears it sounded like a horrified scream.

"He's frozen."

CHAPTER 23

*L*ily cried out, almost choking on the sound of grief and horror. I knew she was close to Logan too, so this would be a doubly painful blow for her. Tears burned ferociously behind my eyes and I blinked them back.

Kai didn't look any better, her eyes now deep in the hollows of her sockets, dark smudges beneath her lids making her look haunted. I wished I could make it all go away.

Wishful thinking.

Not helping.

I studied the room in which Logan was being held, projecting inside for greater detail. Some kind of biological research lab. Wraparound shelving and tables, glass-fronted cupboards filled with bottles of chemicals. And dozens of medical machines.

Omega had certainly spared no expense.

The contraption keeping Logan frozen looked like something out of a bad sci-fi movie, all metal and blue glowing lights. His face was half hidden behind the glass window, his skin gray and shimmering with ice crystals.

Beside the window sat a keypad and a panel showing oxygen

levels and temperature fluctuation. Below the panel was a white label bearing a warning that stilled my heart.

"How the hell do we get him out of there?" Kai's whispered question shattered the tense silence, bringing me back to her side.

"I had a look," I shook my head, hating to be the bearer of such horrible news. "It's very secure. It also has a self-destruct. We need to enter the correct code or the cryo-chamber will kill him."

Kai stared at me, her eyes wide, her skin white as the blood drained from her face. She glanced back at Logan, horror in her eyes making her look like the living dead.

"Kai?" I asked, wanting to pull her free from what I suspected was a spiral into helplessness. I wouldn't blame her either. This was too much for most people to handle. "What do we do?" I urged, hoping to pull her from her grief.

She only took a moment to think before shifting her gaze to mine. "There's someone that may be able to help us," Kai said, her voice shaky. "He's at my parent's place at Tukats. Bring him here as fast as possible. I think he may be the only person who can crack the code without tripping the self-destruct."

I nodded, satisfied that we were moving, that we now had something to do that could get Logan free. "Be back in a sec."

I jumped straight to Kai's home in Tukats, landing in the front hall. A step into the living room revealed a roaring fire but an empty room. The kitchen, gleaming in chrome and wood, gave me the same answer.

I projected and scanned the house finding the study occupied by a young man who gave off not a single sign of being alive.

Kai had a vamp living in her home?

I couldn't waste time wondering if my friend had finally lost it. Instead, I jumped to the study and appeared beside him.

"Sorry to disturb," I said startling the boy. He flinched so hard that his chair slid back a whole foot. I held a hand up. "Sorry to frighten you. Kai sent me. We need to hurry."

He took one look at me, grabbed his laptop and threw a black rucksack bag over his shoulder. I jumped him to Kai, reappearing as Lily paced up and down in front of Logan's prison. The vamp-boy held his stomach, then shifted his free hand to his mouth.

"Geez," he said, his throat hoarse, his eyes scanning his surroundings. "How come that was worse than when Jess took us to—" His jaw clamped shut as he caught sight of Logan in the next room. "Can you get me in there now?" He glanced at me.

I nodded, grabbed his forearm and jumped him into the room, materializing beside the cryo-pod. He flipped the flap of his rucksack open and retrieved a set of cables. Setting his laptop on the floor he connected his keypad to the pod, then focused, his fingers flying over the keys.

I left him there and returned to Kai, still worried about the two girls. Wordlessly, I held out a hand to each of them. They took it just as silently and I jumped them inside the room, landing beside the vamp-boy.

"Aren't we worried about sensors picking up our presence?" Kai asked studying the pod as the vamp typed.

He glanced up for a brief moment. "Don't worry about that. I've disabled the sensors. They only had one at the door to detect people entering the room."

Kai nodded almost absently, as if a single sensor was the least of her problems. I didn't doubt it. Seconds later, she shifted her weight from one foot to the other. "How much longer?" she asked, her expression bordering on desperate.

"Give me a minute." The vamp-boy seemed to understand Kai very well. He kept his tone low and firm, subtly helping her to maintain her calm. "The cryo-process has already begun. Unplugging him now without being super-careful, may hurt him if not kill him."

Kai swallowed and stared at Logan for a moment before

shifting her attention to me. "Is it possible to transport him out of the room to safety?"

I didn't hesitate.

"Yes, I could do that fairly easily as long as I don't have to transport the whole pod. I don't have the energy right now for such a huge jump." I hated to admit it but in such a situation, honesty was best.

The vamp glanced at us. "You don't need to take the pod. As long as you take the wiring and the generator he will survive."

I opened my mouth to agree but a beeping interrupted me. The panel on the pod began to blink and a countdown appeared, ticking off the seconds until something awful happened.

Kai gasped. "Crap. You must have set something off."

"Take him now," said the vamp, his face expressionless.

Before I moved, Kai glanced at me. "As soon as you leave him, come straight back for Lily."

I gave her a nod. "You guys ready?"

After they all agreed, I jumped, carefully landing inside the pod beside Logan. The space was cramped but the design of the chamber was spacious enough to accommodate the two of us, allowing me to materialize without morphing with Logan's cells.

It only took a moment to grab hold of him, and to sense and hold onto the generator and the cables connected to it.

Then I jumped us to Kai's family home.

CHAPTER 24

We arrived inside the kitchen. I was thinking ahead, choosing the tiled floor of the kitchen rather than the wood and carpet in the front hall.

Holding Logan carefully as I solidified, I laid his frozen form on the floor. Then checked for a pulse. Still nothing, but already with the change in temperature, the skin on Logan's face was beginning to glisten as the ice melted.

I left him there and went straight back for the girl. "Lily, you can come and look after Logan for me?"

Lily gave Kai a glance, which could have meant either who-the-hell-is-she-to-give-me-orders or are-you-going-to-be-okay-alone. Still, she said nothing as I whisked her away, landing beside Logan.

Lily gasped and sank to the knees, her pants soaking up water from a melting Logan. Lily checked his temperature with the back of her hand and muttered something under her breath.

"He's thawing out fast."

"Hopefully not too fast," said Lily as she checked the rest of his limbs for ice residue.

I stepped closer. "If he's no longer frozen, perhaps we can put him on a bed somewhere?" I knelt beside Lily, helping her get her hand beneath Logan.

She looked up at me. "Are you going to jump him?"

I shook my head. "No. I don't think he can handle a jump like that in his condition. As much as it looks easy, it takes a toll on the body. And mid-thaw we could end up only damaging him further."

Lily nodded slowly, then grabbed Logan by the waist. She looked about to lift him when I said, "Wait. I'll help."

"I don't need your help," she said, then immediately looked contrite. "I'm sorry. I didn't mean it that way."

I waved her off, not needing an apology when things were this intense.

But Lily touched my arm. "I am sorry. I only mean that I'm a walker. I'll use my shifter strength to help me carry him upstairs. You can go back to fetch Kai."

I nodded, noticing she didn't say anything about fetching Anjelo. In fact, she seemed oddly calm about it, almost accepting —which was more than strange.

I left Lily and returned to Kai, feeling the pull of fatigue, the distraction of everything else going on in my life.

"Are you okay?" Kai asked, looking at me, concerned.

I waved a hand at the question. "What's going on?"

The vamp, having put his stuff away, rose to stand beside me, the very same question reflected in his eyes.

"Anjelo." Kai swallowed. From her demeanor it was clear she was struggling not to cry. "He's somewhere here in this facility. When I last saw him on the monitors in Storm's apartment, it didn't look good."

I nodded although I wasn't confident that I'd return with a positive answer. "Let me go and have a look. I might be a few minutes because I have no idea how big the place is."

Fortunately I didn't have to go too far. They'd kept the younger walker a few halls away, in a room almost identical to Logan's. From the looks of it, they'd been ready to take him away, probably to the morgue. Or worse.

When I materialized beside Kai, she gave me an almost grateful look, as if I'd returned in time to save her, from what I wasn't sure.

She reached for me, and the vamp followed suit. I jumped her to Anjelo's side.

After a moment of silence, Kai looked at the vamp. "Are there any sensors in here?"

He glanced down at the laptop tucked in the crook of his elbow and gave a nod. "But it doesn't matter now. The facility is empty. There's no sign of anyone around."

"Maybe they found out that Storm has been taken?" Kai shifted her body, seeming reluctant to look at Anjelo. Then she straightened and moved toward the gurney. Putting two fingers to the boy's neck—which I already knew was a waste of time— she waited to hear a heartbeat.

I'd understood that walkers possessed heightened senses, hearing being one of them. And yet she still performed the task.

I didn't even want to imagine what she was going through. But there was one thing I did know about Kailin Odel, I knew she'd be blaming herself.

The vamp's voice pulled her from wherever her thoughts had gone. "How long has he been dead?" His eyes were large and round as he stared at the dead boy.

Kai's fingers folded into fists. "He's very cold," her voice shook, "Maybe it's just the temperature of the room."

I knew better, but I didn't say anything.

She took a shaky breath. "Someone came into the room," she said. "And unstrapped him, and took him away on a gurney. But I can't be sure that he was alive at that time."

"He could already have been dead when you were watching him being taken away," I said softly. Kai had to come to terms with the reality of the boy's death. Easier said than done when she'd only just recently lost her own sister.

But she turned her back on me, her attention focused solely on the dead boy.

I let Kai sit for a few minutes with the body, but as time drifted by, the danger of being discovered by Omega increased.

I touched her shoulder, curving an arm around her. "Kai," I said softly. "We should get out of here."

Kai looked at me, her green eyes sparkling with tears. She blinked them back and smoothed her hands down the sides of her pants, taking a quick shaky breath. Then she nodded and gave me a half-smile.

I'd never admired her more. For her strength, her conviction, her ability to put the needs of all others before her own.

I jumped Kai, her vamp hacker and Anjelo to Kai's kitchen, too late remembering that Logan had melted all over the floor leaving the place more than a little wet.

Lily had left a small trail of droplets in her wake as she'd taken him upstairs.

My head spun after the effort of jumping three people at the same time and I was surprised that my nose wasn't bleeding.

Kai spoke, her voice bringing me back to the present. "Help me get him to the smaller lounge." She cocked her chin up the hall, and I reached for the body.

I jumped him quickly to the room Kai had indicated, and settled him onto the sofa. I tucked a few cushions beneath his head and straightened to watch him. He could have been sleeping, so peaceful was his face.

I only hoped his afterlife was at least half as peaceful as his expression implied.

Taking a deep breath, I returned to Kai's side. "I've left him on one of the sofas. It didn't seem right to leave him on the floor."

Kai nodded, her expression hopeless and weary. As much as I wanted to help, I needed to get back and contact Saleem. Find out what the hell he was doing.

I felt guilty now, leaving her for personal reasons, but I had little choice. "I hate to desert you, but I really have to go now."

Kai threw me a bright smile, a little ray of happiness in a bleak time. "Thank you, Mel," she said. "If you need me, I'm there." Though her voice didn't convey her gratitude her eyes did well enough. I didn't need any more than that.

I leaned toward Kai, gave her a quick hug and a teary smile.

Then I jumped back home.

I landed in my living room, my mind in a tailspin.

I'd kept it together all this while, but now that it was all over, the reality hit me. Storm had abducted Lily. Storm had killed Anjelo.

Storm had frozen Logan in a cryo-chamber for some reason I couldn't fathom.

I sank onto the sofa, my legs shaking so much they could no longer bear my weight. Glancing around the room, as if grasping desperately for something to hold onto, I took a shuddering breath.

Focus.

I needed to focus my mind, to get a plan in place, find out what I needed to know in a methodical and level-headed manner.

Never mind that all I wanted was to interrogate him myself.

I stiffened, thinking about all the people that could have been responsible for setting the poltergeist on me.

Could Storm be one of them? The one person I'd never thought to obtain samples from.

But even if he wasn't the one responsible for my own issues, he was still instrumental in inflicting pain and suffering on so many others. Even people I care about.

But I didn't get time to think.

My phone beeped and I barely registered the time as just after 1am. A message from Erik appeared on the screen.

Ready when you are. Can you pick me up at the bar in Venice?

Showtime.

CHAPTER 25

I got to my feet, grabbed my satchel and yelled for Steph.

She came running downstairs, hair mussed and face puffy with sleep.

"What happened?" her eyes were wide.

"I have to go. Erik's meeting me and we're heading to Hong Kong. I've got that appointment with Elise and hopefully we'll have some decent progress on this case."

"Don't move," Steph yelled, turned on her heel and sped up the stairs. I waited as she flew to the comms room, puttered around in there, then came thudding back down to me.

"Here," she handed me a small black device, then bent over, struggling for breath, and waving a hand at me as if the movement would fill in the blanks, "signal jammer . . . for cameras and phones . . . thought you might need it . . ."

"Thanks. Brilliant idea," I grinned as she finally straightened.

Steph nodded. "I'm just hoping he was wrong about captive Agamas elves."

"You and me both, girl. You and me both."

❧

I met Erik in the same shadowed booth we'd so recently occupied. I only materialized long enough to project first to find a good spot and grab hold of him.

I jumped him to a deserted hallway beyond the reception area at the Garner-Royal Sun Hotel in Hong Kong. The irony that the hotel technically belonged to Erik wasn't lost on either of us.

We hurried to the reception desk and booked the cheapest room I could find, posing as brother and sister on vacation. I'd had enough of luxury the last time I'd been here, and I wasn't about to indulge my expense account for a mere hour's sleep, if that.

I headed upstairs with Erik in tow, the boy's eyes remaining focused on his phone as we rode the glass elevator. I studied Erik Garner during the ride. Gangly limbs, pale skin, a gamer or a nerd. Smart, bright, caring. And I found myself wondering how any mother could turn a blind eye to a child like him.

I hid a smile as I realized he wasn't that much younger than I was, yet he seemed to still belong in childhood.

We entered the room and I dropped my satchel beside the bed. Erik grabbed a piece of hotel stationery and a pen, and proceeded to draw a rough sketch of the floor-plan of Elise's floor.

After we went over a tentative plan, I got to my feet. "Anything else we need to do? Should we be scoping the place out before we get there? You know what you need to do?"

He nodded, ruffling his hair as he spun his phone on his fingers. "We've been over this before. Let's get something to eat." He was beginning to get short-tempered and I understood.

Young people wanted things to happen quick-fast. And considering he could phase, I didn't think he'd ever let things come to him. He appeared to be the kind of kid who'd go out and get what he wanted when he wanted.

Then I stiffened. "What about cameras inside her office?"

Erik smirked. "Mother would not like cameras catching her at her most vulnerable" he shook his head, "trust me . . . no cameras inside the office."

I nodded slowly, relieved. "Okay. You should get something to eat. *I* am going to see if I can get some rest.

I freshened up as Erik called room-service and ordered a burger and fries. Sinking into one of the double beds, I used the eye mask I'd found in the nightstand to shut out the light.

Lying there, I dozed as Erik pieced together his plan and wrote everything down. I'd insisted that he put it all down on paper so I knew exactly what we both needed to do.

This was dangerous

And I had no backup.

No time to call anyone, not even pull in a few favors with Logan or Kai.

Logan.

I'd forgotten about Logan and his current frozen state. Things had avalanched since I'd left Kai and I hoped she and Lily were handling Anjelo's death okay.

Plus I worried even more about Saleem. Alone in Mithras without backup.

But what could I do but wait to hear from him? Other than running off to Mithras to find him, I had little choice *but* to wait.

And deal with things on my own.

I knew Tanaka was around the corner, so I probably could get his help if need be. I only hoped I wouldn't have to. The fewer people involved the better.

Thankfully, I'd come well-equipped, my satchel filled with all the necessary weapons and ammunition.

I must've fallen asleep, because what seemed like seconds later, Erik was gently shaking me by the shoulder.

"It's time."

I dragged myself off the bed, my hand instinctively going to my nose to check if it had bled.

It had.

Glancing down at the pillow, now soaked with blood, I felt the urge to scream. How much longer could I put up with this?

I got to my feet and rushed off to the bathroom, leaving a very confused Erik staring from the bloodied pillow to me and back again. He hovered in the doorway as I washed my face and cleaned the bloodstains off my nose.

"Are you okay?" he asked softly, his face dark with worry.

I dried off and turned to face him. "I'm fine. You don't need to worry. It was the jump from Venice to Hong Kong that did it for me." Not to mention jumping three people at once, plus all those jumps so close to together carrying people around.

But I figured a little bit of information wouldn't hurt.

He lifted an eyebrow, folded his hands and leaned against the doorjamb. "I thought you were a powerful SoulTracker?"

He was trying to be facetious, but I could see that he was worried.

I nodded. "I just haven't been too well in the last few weeks. If I jump too many times within a short period, I tend to get nosebleeds. It's not a big deal."

He frowned. "Are you sure? I don't need you to come with me, you know."

I shook my head. "No way in hell I'm going to let you go alone. If I felt unwell at all, I'd tell you. I wouldn't jeopardize the mission in any way."

He straightened and nodded, appearing satisfied with my answer as he turned and headed deeper into the room. I followed him, grabbed my bag and packed everything, slipping my dagger into my boot and checking to ensure that my gun was loaded.

This was one of those missions where I really had no idea what I was up against. It tended to get a little complicated for weapons and ammunition. Stab a demon in the gut, and he'll keep coming. Some would need decapitation to stay down.

And what do I remove his head from his shoulders with? I can't exactly walk around with two-foot swords that could do the job well.

Then there was the ammunition. What could bring down a demon would not necessarily incapacitate a dark elf, let alone kill it. Pity none of my ammunition would work on my evil spirit.

I bit back a bitter smile and slung the satchel over my shoulder slapping Erik on the shoulder.

"You ready for this?"

He nodded but refused to look at me. I sidestepped into his line of sight and peered at his face. "There is no shame in being nervous. This is a really big deal. And it's not easy for anyone to face their parent down in a situation like this."

He gave me a grateful smile. "Thank you for being there for me. For taking my side."

I shook my head. "It's not really a matter of sides, Erik. Good and right always win."

I hid my tiny flinch as I said those words. Good and right didn't always win.

Sometimes good and right lost big time.

CHAPTER 26

*I*t was a dull evening, but the murky sky up above the tops of the high-rises were barely visible. The city was already filled with neon lights blinking and flickering in every direction. The beauty of the Hong Kong sky at sunset was a combination of man meets concrete and garish neon lights.

Strangely enough it worked, giving the entire skyline an eerie, almost magical atmosphere. Down on the streets though, the magic disappeared, leaving us with the cab-infested, people-infested street-party and nothing beautiful to admire for miles.

Erik and I lurked around on the street opposite the entrance to Trinity Towers, his mother's office building. I scanned faces while we talked. Then I leaned against the wall and beckoned Erik closer.

He shifted toward me, pretending to give me a hug. It was the only way I could project into the building without anyone seeing my face. Although my eyes didn't go all white the way Samuel's did when I projected, my expression did change.

According to Steph, I looked as if I'd partied with Synthe, the latest walker drug.

I scanned the ground floor of the building, and floated toward the elevator shaft. Inside, I studied the rectangular metal box and was glad to see that the interior of the shaft had been constructed in order to help maintenance workers move up and down. There were plenty of ladders and handholds.

I returned to my body and gave Erik a run down. Then we headed down the street and around the corner, looking for the nearest shadow-filled alleyway.

The place was filled with people, walking, talking, and eating, and I couldn't distinguish between resident and tourist. I gave Erik a glance, a little worried now that we couldn't find a place that was quiet enough to disappear into.

"We should have stayed at the hotel and jumped directly from there," I murmured.

He held my shoulder and tipped his head at the entrance to a small hotel. An exclusive boutique hotel, all glass chandeliers and dark plum upholstery, wasn't the best choice but Erik and I entered, smiling at each other as if we were enjoying a night on the town.

Thankfully, the reception desk was busy and we snuck past the gaggle of guests checking in, and headed down the hall toward the restrooms. We ended up ducking into the ladies' room at the last minute, and I hid a smile as Erik made a disgusted face.

"Oh, please. At least women don't have urinals. Now, that's disgusting." I snorted.

He opened his mouth to respond, then closed it.

I took a firm hold of his waist and gave him a nod, then jumped straight into the elevator shaft inside the Towers. I held onto him tightly, and thankfully he managed to retain his balance long enough so that, when we materialized, he could secure his footing along the ledge that ran around the base of the elevator box.

"Are you good?" I whispered. He merely nodded, his lips twisting. But I had no time to baby him. If he was feeling nauseous from the jump, there was nothing I could do about it right now. Not even if I'd wanted to.

I rummaged in my bag with my free hand and retrieved the camera, handing it over to him carefully. He looped the strap over his neck and said, "Please be careful. The woman is like a shark in the water. She'll sense something is wrong, so *be* careful."

I nodded and patted him on the shoulder. "You be careful, too. And just remember, if you have any trouble with the elf send me a text. Try and assure him that we'll do everything possible to keep his daughter safe. If she's being held, we'll extract her. If he doesn't believe you, tell him we'll send him proof. And explain to him that we need her caught on tape, making him create the diamonds."

Erik rolled his eyes. "We've been all over this already, Mel."

I shook my head, ignored him and said, "After I meet with your mother, I'll go in search of the elf's daughter. Hopefully I can find her and secure her location fast, so you can placate him."

He nodded and I didn't give him any more time to question the plan. I jumped back to the restroom, straightened my clothing and strolled back out into the foyer. The concierge gave me a suspicious, haughty glare and I picked up the pace, giving him little chance to run after me. I was pretty sure walk-ins weren't allowed to avail themselves of the facilities, especially not in hotels as posh as this.

I hurried along the busy street, barely seeing the people around me. I had so many things on my mind that I was seriously considering not taking on any more cases until my own issues were resolved.

I reached the glass high-rise building that housed Elise Garner's Hong Kong offices, and went straight to the reception desk on the ground floor to report in and receive my visitor's badge. I headed to the bank of elevators, giving the button a quick stab.

As soon as the doors opened, I stepped inside and punched Elise's floor. Then I used the signal jammer Steph had given me and hoped it worked. I couldn't afford for the elevator camera to catch me in action.

Projecting quickly, I peered beyond the metal doors and the high-end elevator carriage.

Erik, hung onto the outside of the elevator, holding on tightly as it surged upward sending his hair flying. I made a mental note to flick him a quick text, letting him know that I was in the elevator.

It worried me that he had to hold on while the car shot up thirty-six floors, and I prayed he'd be safe. A part of me prayed he'd just phase himself to safety if something went wrong.

The ride up to Garner International was both faster than I expected, and slower than I wanted. Something about the woman put me on edge, and I wasn't looking forward to this meeting.

Give me a demon any day.

I stepped off the elevator, my low-heeled boots sinking deep into plush carpets—a deep coffee color this time. The woman seemed to have a thing for overly plush carpets.

Before I left, I did a quick projection to confirm that Erik had moved away from the car, and had climbed along the side of the shaft. I frowned, hoping he knew where he was going.

A second receptionist watched me from behind a long white desk, her expression cool and almost disdainful.

The woman got to her feet, tossed her long black ponytail over her shoulder and straightened her short skirt, which had ridden up, revealing a little too much thigh.

"Miss Morgan, I presume?" she asked, one of her painted eyebrows lifting slightly.

I forced myself to smile and nod and follow when she beckoned me through a pair of gigantic golden doors. Carved with dragons and depicting legions of soldiers at war, it seemed extremely out of place in a diamond company headquarters.

Still this was Hong Kong, and it was probably Elise's homage to the citizens of her adopted country.

More plush carpets, and when we entered a small waiting room—more like a very luxurious lounge—the receptionist waved her hand in the direction of a white leather sofa.

I took a seat, resolving to control my temper and to be patient. No matter what. Too many chess pieces were riding on this one conversation.

A few moments later, the inner door opened and the young girl exited, pausing to wave a hand in the direction of the office. As I walked over the threshold I caught a glimpse of the expression on Elise Garner's face as she watched her assistant leave. A glance over my shoulder confirmed the sultry glance was shared.

So that's the way it is.

I schooled my features and headed over to the pair of deep red leather armchairs in front of Elise's desk.

She stood with her back to floor-to-ceiling windows providing a view onto the Hong Kong night. The view wasn't very much different to the one that I'd had from Darius's apartment two days ago.

Erik's mother sat and shifted her chair forward, resting her elbows on her gleaming redwood desk. "To what do I owe the honor, Miss Morgan?" she asked, a cool smile on her face. She had to be wondering why I'd returned so quickly.

I smiled. "Don't worry, I'm not here to tell you that I don't want the job any longer."

She let out a cool laugh, but I didn't miss the flicker of relief in her eyes. "That was the least of my concerns." She sat back, relatively relaxed and studied me.

"How can I help you? Is there information you need to help you get this job done?" Then she paused and frowned. "Has there been a problem with the payment?" She seemed annoyed as if pre-empting the problem.

I shook my head. "No, not at all. In fact, I would have preferred not to have received payment as yet. At any rate, I've sequestered the funds just in case things don't pan out."

She raised her eyebrows. "What do you mean 'in case things don't pan out'?"

"I've just come from Venice, and there are a few things weighing on my mind regarding this case."

"I see," she said, her voice calm and neutral. But the woman's eyes seemed to give away a lot about her emotions.

While she may believe she possessed a poker-face and could control people with a mere look, her glare failed to work on me. "What is it?"

She didn't say it, but I knew she was hoping I wasn't about to waste any more of her time.

"I do believe there's more to this robbery than meets the eye. At first I thought your son was attempting to steal the diamonds, maybe to fund his alleged vigilante venture, but after having scanned the store, and viewed the footage, I'm not so sure anymore."

Elise laughed, got to her feet. "I'm not sure how to take the fact that you've gained access to the footage without my permission."

"You hired me on as an investigator, you hired me to find your son. I'm not in the business of asking for help every few seconds, especially when those things are almost trivial, things I could easily obtain myself.

"I have the contacts and can access most anything that I need. I *was* under the impression that was the reason you hired me . . . my efficiency and ability to get the job done." I raised my own eyebrow at her now.

My defiance in the face of her cold haughtiness seemed to have broken through her ice. She gave a deep sigh and then took her seat again. Picking up the phone she spoke, "Catherine can we have two coffees?"

But Catherine cut her off and whatever she'd said to Elise drew an alarming reaction. The skin on Garner's face darkened, and grew tighter, more lined.

She was back up on her feet within a second. As she put the phone down she glanced up at me. "I apologize Ms Morgan, we seem to be having a few issues on the security front. If you wouldn't mind waiting here for me, I'll be back in a few minutes."

She headed out of the office—without even waiting for my response—and closed the door behind her.

"What is it Catherine?"

"Security just called. Something strange was caught on the cameras in the elevator shaft. Anderson thinks he detected some kind of movement. It could be nothing, but we just want to let you know."

"With my son flitting around the world, causing mayhem for me, I hardly think this is nothing. I'll go down and speak to Anderson myself."

I returned to my body, surprised at her dedication to something as minor as security. It only proved to me how afraid the woman was of her son.

And we probably wouldn't have too much time, so I settled in, keeping my back to the door and projected into the interior room.

Erik was having a spirited conversation with a bound elf, at the same time attempting to fix the camera behind a portion of loose paneling.

"I assure you, Raulfir, your daughter will be found and we will do everything in our power to ensure she is safe."

The elf glared at Erik. "All you're going to do is get my daughter killed."

Erik shook his head. "You need to keep your voice down. I'm not sure this room is soundproof."

The elf laughed. "Of course, it's soundproof. Do you think your mother makes it easy for me?"

"How do you know she's my mother?" Erik asked Raulfir, distracted now by the elf's line of questioning.

It was time to give him a bit of a helping hand.

CHAPTER 27

*J*teleported straight into the room causing the elf—
Raulfir—to flinch as I appeared right beside him.

Erik gave me a relieved glance. "Can you please speak to him? Got to get this camera situated."

I knelt beside the elf, regretting that I was unable to help him remove his restraints. "We don't have a lot of time," I watched Erik as his fingers deftly intertwined wires within the panel, "Elise will be back any second now. Erik, you must've set off their motion sensor in the elevator shaft—they're all swarming the shaft looking for an intruder."

He gave me a worried glance, but continued twisting wires and setting up the camera.

I looked at the elf. "My highest priority is to find your daughter and take her away to safety. I promise you . . . I will take good care of her. My name is Mel Morgan. I'm a tracker. My job is to look for missing people. Even if your daughter is not being held in the building, I will still find her."

The elf frowned. "Do you think they're holding Silvanya here?"

I didn't need to answer. He'd figured it out all on his own. Just the way Erik had done. The elf's shoulders sagged and he sank against the backrest of the chair. "I should have known not to trust her."

I sighed and patted his shoulder. "Nothing we can do about that now. What we would like you to do is help us put her in jail where she belongs. Your daughter . . . Silvanya . . . will be fine. I just wanted to assure you that our intentions are good, and if you could please cooperate with Erik. I apologize for not taking you to safety immediately, but do you think you could find it possible to help us trap her?"

The elf stared at me for a long moment, his gray eyebrows bunched as he mulled over my words. Then he inhaled sharply. "I'm Raulfir, King of Kil'rith and Beyond." He inclined his head while I tried to absorb the fact that we had royalty on our hands —royalty that we want to keep in Elise's cell. "What would you have me do? Or refrain from doing?" he asked, straightening his shoulders stiffly.

I blinked for a moment while Erik and I exchanged a worried glance.

The elf chuckled. "If you are concerned about my status and title, please stop. By now, my position back home would have been taken over by my son, which means that, technically, I'm a mere co-regent. In absentia."

More confusing Elf politics. But I made a mental note to research the geography and politics of the White Elf realms.

With time running out I couldn't stand on ceremony. Giving him a respectful nod, I said, "I need for you to do as Elise instructs for now. At most, a couple days."

He nodded, his eye narrowing as he considered what I was asking of him.

Freedom so close and yet so far.

"Give it a few hours—just until we can locate and retrieve Silvanya—then begin to resist her. Don't take it too far because I don't want her killing you in the process. But we need it all caught on camera to give us something concrete. We need proof in order to put her away."

He smiled coldly. "I understand. And do not worry. You will get your fodder. The woman is a menace." He shifted his shoulder and glanced at his arm, indicating that he wanted me to see something.

I lifted the sleeve of his cream robe and sucked in a harsh breath. His skin had been branded—almost every inch of it—the surface now tight and shiny, covered in scars that would likely never fade.

Even Elf magic would be unlikely to heal his scarring.

I held my tongue and got to my feet, giving the Elf King a nod. Then with a quick projection, I found that Elise was on her way up.

"I have to go. Erik. Get yourself out of here as soon as possible."

I jumped back into the office, landing safely in my armchair and was just straightening my jacket when Elise entered the room again. I relaxed, glad that she didn't have cameras in her office.

"So what is it you think is going on?" Elise sat back down, and faced me, her expression neutral and back down to business. "Why is it necessary for you to come all the way to Hong Kong to speak to me about this when a phone call would have been sufficient?"

I raised an eyebrow, appearing annoyed. "Well . . . I particularly do not like lies, and I do not like suspecting that I'm being played."

She pursed her lips as she considered my words, then leaned back with an admiring smile.

"I have to admit that from the moment I met you I've admired your attitude. It's good to be a strong woman. Pity that people don't like strong women, nor do they like women who speak their mind." She sighed and sat forward. "There is more to this case than I've let on. I'm sure you've suspected as much if you're here."

I nodded but didn't speak, leaving the floor to my client. Like her son she seemed on edge, very likely to stop talking if I said the wrong thing.

"My son didn't just run away. He left because I refused to leave my business to him," her sigh was filled with sadness, "He'd thought he'd inherit it all when his father died. And when he understood that that was the last thing I'd ever do, he threw a fit. You have to understand my son has always been the do-gooder. The Greenpeace-humanitarian-I-love-the-whole-world-kind of boy. And the problem with him is people *will* fall for his bullshit —he's very convincing. He believes I'm involved in something nefarious and underhanded."

She let out a laugh and got to her feet, her thoughts focused on her son. I doubt she even realized that she'd begun to pace, revealing to me how upset she was.

"And are you?" I asked. I'd already gathered she wasn't about to spill anything important. I didn't really care because this whole meeting was about giving Erik an opportunity to plant the camera.

And that was done.

Elise smiled, nodding to herself before she faced me. "And that's a very good question. The answer to that is no. I would never jeopardize everything my husband built. I'm not sure what Erik's objective is, but he will never get this business."

"So what exactly do you think he's going to do?"

"Like Venice, he'll continue to create problems with each store. Continuing robberies will make it appear to the general public that our stores lack security," she paused, then met my gaze, "Maybe even steal from me."

I shifted and slid my hand into my jacket pocket, withdrawing the black velvet case containing the pink diamond. I placed it on the desk in front of me without saying a word.

She reached for it without a word and flipped the case open. Elise paled and the contours of her face stood out in contrast. "Where did you get that?"

I didn't answer. Instead I said, "I believe you know what this is."

She scowled. "It's a pink diamond."

"That's not what I meant."

She didn't respond.

"It's a blood diamond." Her eyes flitted from the stone to my face, then back again. Her muscles were stiff, tense as if the stone would at any moment turn into a spitting cobra. "And it was found on your premises."

Elise walked slowly toward her seat and sat, the movement controlled and equally slow. "What are you trying to accuse me of?"

I shrugged. "Nothing. I just wanted to warn you that it looks like someone is trying to set you up." A load of bullshit if I ever heard one. It was my save, so I hoped she'd take the bait.

Her face relaxed, and her shoulders slumped just a fraction, enough to let me know that she believed herself in the clear.

She nodded rapidly. "I believe that's quite possible."

"And do you think your son would do such a thing? Plant a blood diamond in your store so you'd be arrested?" Poor Erik. I was colluding with his mother to put the blame on him.

"I don't think so," she spoke so softly I almost didn't hear her, "I hope not."

I frowned. "Maybe it was the Phaser? I was told he was in the store, apparently chasing away the robbers. If you believe this vigilante is your son, why would he be chasing away suspects?"

She smiled and walked to the desk. "I'm not exactly of the belief that the Phaser is my son. I have to admit I've suspected that was the case, but as yet I haven't seen proof. The thing is, he always seemed to be in the vicinity of an attack on one of my properties. Why that is, is the million-dollar question."

I sat still for a moment and nodded as if taking in everything that she'd said. I'd gathered that Elise was the kind of woman who would both love an audience, and enjoy playing the role of superior mentor.

With a sigh I got to my feet. "I apologize for the sudden meeting. But I'm glad I came. Sounds like you've had a lot on your mind, and hopefully I can help relieve some of that stress. I'm confident your son will return soon, and you'll be able to work things out."

Elise smiled, although her lips remained a thin line. She got to her feet and reached out to shake my hand.

She seemed relaxed and at ease, despite the security threat, despite the burgeoning of her deepest fears.

The woman was a good liar.

She guided me toward the door and handed me over to her assistant. I was well and truly dismissed. Catherine led me to the elevators, like a guard dog wanting to confirm I left the building. Thankfully, she didn't accompany me to the ground floor, just waited until I entered the elevator and the doors closed.

As the elevator descended, I projected into the secret room, hoping Erik had gotten himself safely out. But he hadn't left yet, and seemed to be fiddling with the wires for the camera.

What the hell was he still doing?

In her office, Elise was flipping through a stack of folders when she turned her head and stared at bookshelf which hid her torture chamber.

Was it possible that she'd heard something?

No. Erik had mentioned soundproofing.

I shook my head impatient for the elevator to reach the ground floor and spit me out. I headed out of the foyer and then onto the street, instinct urging me to run. I had to force myself to slow down, aware of the cameras all around me.

Crossing the street, I hurried around the corner and ducked into a little cafe. I headed through the throng of people, hoping nobody would see me as I went straight for the telephone tucked into a back corner.

A soon as I slipped behind the screen I jumped to the hidden room, grabbed hold of Erik, barely noticing that he was finally twisting the last screw in place. Raulfir met my gaze, his eyes filled with understanding. I didn't wait to see anything else, just held on and teleported us back into our hotel room.

As I deposited Erik inside the room, I felt a pang of regret for having left the elf . . . Raulfir behind. Still I wondered what he was in for now, especially since—if I had anything to say about it —Elise would soon be without his daughter.

Erik stumbled then regained his footing, spinning around to look at me, a satisfied grin on his face. A smile that disappeared the moment he set eyes on my face.

"Shit." He stared at my nose and pointed.

Groaning, I reached for a wad of Kleenex, tipped my head back and dabbed at my nose to clean up the mess.

The room spun and I refrained from closing my eyes. It usually made the vertigo worse. But my body seemed confused, as if I was still getting my footing.

Blinking as I straightened my neck, I became aware that the room was still spinning around me. I sank on the nearest bed as carefully as I could, reluctant to show Erik my weakness.

The last thing I needed was his doubt. Or his loss of confidence.

Done cleaning up, I squashed the tissues into a ball and tossed it into the trash can.

Then I turned to a very silent Erik and said, "We need to get to the daughter as soon as possible. You never know when Elise would decide to move her for security reasons."

Erik nodded, although he still didn't look convinced as he stared at my face.

I shifted and lay on my back, looking over at him. "I'm going to project. It's going to take a while; the building is quite big."

Erik hesitated. "Is that wise? So soon after . . ." He waved at my nose.

He had a point. But I couldn't afford to waste any more time.

"I'll be fine," I said softly, giving him an encouraging smile.

He said nothing, just grabbed more tissues and handed it to me without a word.

CHAPTER 28

*I*rritated, I swiped hard at my nose, not caring that I was leaving it bruised and red.

I sank into the ether and projected into the high-rise building. Like many of the Hong Kong skyscrapers, this one was no less impressive with its glass walls and five-sided design, it looked modern and sleek.

No surprise Elise Garner had decided this particular building would suit the nature, and the clientele, of her business.

I focused on the top floor, scanning each room, each corridor and office and slowly descended through the building. Thank goodness projection wasn't as bad a stress on my body as actual teleportation. Even while scanning the building, I was getting much-needed rest.

Hopefully my cells would regenerate fast enough because once we find Silvanya we'd have to move our asses.

The Garner International floor was clear, and Elise was back in her office flipping through some paperwork with Catherine. I wondered what she'd think if she knew she was being watched.

When Elise raised a hand and slid it along the inside of

Catherine's thigh, and then further up her skirt, I got the hell out of there. I certainly didn't want to become an ethereal voyeur.

Not now, not ever.

I wondered if Erik knew about his mother's sexual preferences, and if that was maybe a point of contention for them.

Pushing the thought out of my mind, I focused on the job at hand. I descended further through the building, confirming that none of those occupants currently in the structure, were Silvanya, the elf girl.

Wait. That should be Silvanya the Elf Princess.

How'd I miss that?

King Raulfir had been adamant that she be found and I was just as determined to find her. Raulfir seemed to believe that anyone held in captivity by Elise Garner would not survive for too long.

And I was inclined to agree with him.

As luck would have it, I ended up finding Silvanya in the basement. And I wasn't sure if that luck was of the good persuasion.

I finally drifted below the lowest parking-deck to a basement level, locked away behind steel doors. It housed heat pumps and air conditioning generators, as well as other metal equipment I couldn't identify.

Skating along the rabbit-warren of the corridors, I sensed a change in the ether, a throbbing of energy that was unlike anything a mere human could generate.

A set of double metal doors up ahead shimmered with energy which seemed to push against the steel. Locked and bolted from the outside, it certainly looked capable of holding a prisoner.

I projected inside the room, pausing at the entrance to gauge the situation. The room wasn't large, no more than twenty square feet. Empty of furniture, the only thing that occupied the floor was an iron cage.

Silvanya, Elf Princess, sat in the cage, a stubborn defiance in the set of her spine.

A single guard paced a foot from me, swearing under his breath.

Silvanya was smiling, and as I drew closer the condition of her bloodied nose became starkly clear.

We were a matched pair.

I frowned and stared at the guard who was busy waving his hands around and staring at his damaged fists, fueled by frustration and probably fear.

I couldn't imagine the excuse he'd have to come up with to explain to Elise how he'd lost the elf princess. Especially when she'd been safely behind bars the entire the time.

Returning to my body, I opened my eyes and inhaled sharply.

Erik stood from the chair where he'd been sitting, elbows resting on his knees, shoulders hunched over while he kept an eye on me.

I gave him a nod, then got to my feet.

"I found her."

CHAPTER 29

A smile curved Erik's lips.

He'd been rather subdued since we'd returned to the hotel room and I was beginning to worry he was having doubts.

He leaned excitedly toward me. And I had to push him out of the way as I took a step toward my satchel.

"So what's the plan. Are we going in to get her?"

I shook my head. "I don't have the energy to transport two people at the same time. You're going to have to stay behind. It's a pretty simple process, though. I jump, grab her and take her straight to my house in Chicago. I'll have someone watch her there, and I'll return for you."

There must've been a clear apology in my tone because he was already nodding where he'd usually be fighting me for a chance to do his part. I was glad that he understood, glad too as I didn't have the time or the energy for an argument.

My body felt numb with fatigue, limbs wobbled like jello, bones throbbing with constant pain. I was more tired than I'd ever been on a case.

Or in my life.

My heart still ached every time I thought about Anjelo and Logan.

Blinking away tears I focused on Erik. "Oh, can I borrow your Phaser hoodie?"

Erik grinned, grabbed it from the bed and handed it over. "I like the way you think."

I smiled and patted his shoulder, giving it a quick reassuring squeeze. Then I projected into the basement room, arriving behind the guard. I had to ensure the coast was clear.

I'd already scanned the cell for cameras and had found one in the far-left corner. With great care, I materialized directly behind him so his body would shield me from the camera.

I was glad I'd taken the time to wear Erik's Phaser hoodie. It would give Elise cause to think the vigilante had taken Silvanya.

Grabbing hold of the guard, I jumped him to the roof of the building and disappeared, leaving him alone and confused.

I teleported straight back to the basement, materializing inside the metal cage in front of the girl, keeping my back to the camera.

"Please don't be afraid. I'm here to take you to safety," I said, hoping she would understand me. All too often we made the assumption that other magical races would understand our languages. More often than not, that wasn't the case. But seeing that her father had understood me perfectly well, I didn't think I needed to worry.

She smiled and nodded. "Thank you."

I pointed at her face. "What happened?"

She lifted a single arched brow. "The guard thought he could get frisky with me."

"What did you do to deserve that honor?" I peered at her bloody nose.

She grinned and cupped her hand, then made a grabbing, upward motion.

No need for words.

I liked her already.

I held out my hand and the second she took hold of it I jumped her straight back into our living room.

Silvanya swayed on her feet, and I held tightly onto her waist, helping her slowly to the sofa. "Stay there for a bit. Teleporting has that effect sometimes."

She nodded and sank back against the cushions, her pale hair framing her face in much the same way as her father's. I was pretty sure she wasn't going anywhere anytime soon.

Heading out into the hall to the bottom of the stairs, I yelled for Steph, sighing with relief as the stamping of her feet echoed down to me as she hurried from the comms room.

"What happened?" she said, her voice loud and concerned as she scrambled down the stairs toward me. "Are you okay?"

I batted her searching hands away. "I'm fine, but we have a guest." I glared at her as she rolled eyes, but she schooled her features when I pointed a warning finger at her.

Steph, for all her complaints, was a wonderful host to the lost people I brought home. I had nothing to worry about when she looked after them. Having a comfortable, homely environment to house them in while they transitioned from the trauma of their ordeal, from captivity to freedom, was always helpful.

We entered the living room, and Steph gave Silvanya a short wave. "Hey. I'm Steph. Just tell me if you need anything."

Silvanya smiled back and introduced herself simply with her name, leaving out her titles or any reference to her royal lineage. Steph mentioned something about tea while I scanned my phone for any updates from Saleem or Kai. When I looked up she'd disappeared.

I shifted to the doorway, drawing a curious glance from Silvanya.

"I've got to fetch Erik. I'll be right back."

Before she could say a word, I jumped back to the hotel room, where Erik was sitting on the bed staring at his phone.

Again I was taken with how young he looked for his age. I had to keep reminding myself of the fact.

"You ready?" I asked, startling him so much that he flinched.

"What the-" His eyes widened and then he scowled. As he got to his feet, I hooked an arm around his waist and jumped him back to the living room.

With our arrival, Silvanya cringed, moving away from Erik as he materialized beside me. She gave him a fearful glance then looked away.

Erik hesitated then took a step back, sitting slowly on the larger sofa as far away from the princess as the furniture arrangement would allow.

Steph walked into the room with a cup of tea in her hand. She headed for Silvanya, handed over the hot drink carefully, then glanced at me, giving Erik a pointed look.

I shrugged and would have spoken had Erik not leaned forward and said to Silvanya, "You okay?" he shifted closer, "What did she do to you?"

Silvanya's eyes lifted to meet his, eyelashes dark and framing eerie silvery eyes. She stared at him, as if shocked at the question.

"You can tell us what she's done," I said softly. "We're going to make sure that she's apprehended and punished."

The girl nodded but she didn't appear convinced.

I went to sit beside her, maintaining a tiny bit of distance in case she was disturbed by my close proximity. Who knew how her time in captivity would affect her, now or in the future.

"We found your father as well," I said softly, "We were unable to take him to safety immediately, but the plan is to go in and get him as soon as possible. He knows you're safe."

Her gaze snapped to my face, her eyes now round and filling with tears. "Do you swear that he is safe?"

I nodded and so did Erik. "He is. I was with him for a while. He is a very brave man."

Silvanya frowned and she looked from Erik's face to mine,

her brow furrowing in confusion. "What do you mean . . . brave man? Why haven't you brought him to safety?"

I patted the back of her hand. "He agreed to stay behind to gather evidence against Elise Garner. We need to catch her in the act."

Silvanya got to her feet and glared at me. "You have no idea what you have done."

I shook my head. "If you explain it to me, then I can understand your concerns better. There's a lot about this case that's really confusing for all of us."

Silvanya leaned forward her expression earnest and scared. "You don't understand. That woman knows where our family lives. She's been holding us, forcing us to do her bidding, because she knows we would do anything to keep our family safe."

"Where is your family?" My heart thudded. Nothing surprised me about Elise Garner, yet each time I heard how low she'd sunk, I felt sicker.

"In Kil'rith, the elf realm. She has exclusive access to the veil between the worlds. She can come and go as she pleases. She's proven it many a time. At first my father refused to help her, but when she returned with the pinky finger of my mother's left-hand, we both knew we had no choice."

My heart tightened enough to hurt and I exchanged shocked glances with Steph and Erik.

"Then it's imperative that we shut her down as fast as possible." I glanced at Steph. "Can you access that camera feed and keep an eye on it twenty-four-seven. We'll take turns watching."

Silvanya began to cry, glaring at me through her tears.

"Why are you doing this to him? Hasn't he been through enough?"

I looked at her sadly. "I'm really sorry, but this was the only way. Your father wanted to help. He knows the consequences if we all do nothing. It's not a mere possibility that when she's ready she may return to enslave more people from your world. It's a definite."

Silvanya sat down and wiped eyes. "When can I go home?" I hesitated, hating that I had to force her to remain here against her will. "You get some rest. You'll be needed here for debriefing after everything is over. And I'm sure you want to wait to see your father?" She gave a small nod. "I'm hoping we can get your father out of captivity and Elise imprisoned in the next couple of days."

"Is there a way to block her access to our world?" Silvanya asked, desperation edging her question.

I nodded. "There must be a way. But she has to be held accountable and imprisoned. Stopping her access to Kil'rith isn't enough." I looked over at Steph. "Steph will look after you. I wish I could stay. I have a few errands that I need to run."

Silvanya nodded, wringing her hands as she turned to face me. "I apologize if I have appeared ungrateful. I understand what you're trying to do. And if my father agreed to do this . . . to help you, it is not my place to object. And I hope you can return him to us safely."

I squeezed her fingers and then gave her a quick hug. Within my embrace, the elf-girl shivered, and I suspected she may be suffering from shock. Likely PTSD, even if she's her own kind of badass.

I released her and went to Steph. "Can you get Chloe here? We'll need her help now."

I sighed, feeling weighed down by it all as my body rebelled against the non-stop crazy of my world.

I glanced out the window at the navy-blue sky, bathed in soft pink and violent red. Dawn was greeting us and yet it felt like all the days had bled into one.

"All these time zone changes are making me a little crazy." I turned to Erik who was back to studying the screen of his phone.

"Come. We should all probably get some rest. I'll show you to a room. You can stay here as long as you want to."

He nodded and got to his feet, giving Silvanya a concerned glance. I knew what he was feeling.

Guilt.

That she'd had to go through such horrors at the hands of his mother. That he'd been unable to stop that horror.

But Silvanya had turned to speak to Steph, her tone low. Already, she appeared to have calmed down and had even smiled a few times as she talked to Steph.

I left them to it and headed upstairs with Erik in tow. One of the best things about this old house was it had more than enough rooms.

I led Erik to one at the furthest end of the hall and opened the door for him. As he entered, he paused on the threshold and turned to look at me. "I don't think I've said this to you, but I'm very grateful for everything you've done for me. Anybody else would've just handed me back to my mother, collected their pay and left."

My lips curled into a fond smile. "Not sure I could have done it any differently. You get some rest and we'll talk later."

He hesitated as if there was something else he wanted to say, but bit his tongue and strode inside in silence.

I sighed stilling the urge to put my arm around him in comfort. He'd only rebuff me. "You don't have to feel guilty about them, you know. What she did is not on you."

He turned and looked away. "Common sense tells me that it isn't. But everything else about the situation makes me feel responsible. Maybe for not stopping it sooner. Maybe for running away and leaving her with full control, with nobody to rein her in, even if it was just to act as her conscience."

I shook my head and leaned against the threshold. "You have to stop blaming yourself. That's the only way you're going to get over this. You've seen Silvanya . . . she'll be fine. She doesn't look like the damsel-in-distress type."

He snorted and smiled, giving me a grateful nod. I waved at him and closed the door, leaving him to get some rest.

It was probably time I got some of my own.

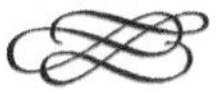

CHAPTER 30

After so many near-mishaps, I navigated the shower the way a soldier moved across a battlefield. The spirit had so far been a very private persecutor, keeping his hauntings just between the two of us.

I'd found leaving my bedroom and bathroom door open, tended to reduce the frequency of his attacks. Not that it was always a possibility what with our intermittent guests.

My shower was only disturbed by a disappearing cake of soap and a narrow miss with a squeeze-bottle of toilet bleach which had taken the place of my shampoo.

Paid to be observant.

I'd dressed in jeans and a burnt orange peasant shirt, and was sliding my knife into my boot when my phone beeped.

I grabbed it from my nightstand and read the message from Natasha.

I found you a Kitsune sorcerer. He's agreed to meet you but because he had so many conditions I negotiated neutral ground. The Sahara Desert. Come as soon as you can. And remember, he's a sorcerer so he's not truly trustworthy.

I raised my eyebrows as I read the message, then texted back for the time and specific location.

I yawned as I left my room, having spent the last hour or so tossing and turning, unable to sleep.

Too wired. Too worried. Too . . . everything.

My slippers slapped the bare wood of the hallway as I headed for the stairs, but when I got to the top of the staircase I froze, staring down at the staircase from which I'd so recently taken a swan dive.

A moment of vertigo kicked me hard in the gut and I found my fingers curling tightly around the balustrade of their own accord, knuckles white, muscles strained.

What the hell?

Was I now afraid of heights or something? Seriously? I couldn't afford any more crazy in my life.

Inhaling a breath filled with hot fury, I descended the stairs, taking each riser one at a time. I made it all the way to the bottom without incident, and released the breath—which was considerably calmer.

Entering the kitchen, the first thing that caught my eye was a plate of freshly-baked muffins. I stopped in my tracks. Not that muffins were confusing. Just the freshly-baked part had me wondering.

This could not possibly be the work of our Stephanie.

I also found a freshly-brewed pot of coffee and poured a cup, while glancing covertly at the baked goods and wondering if they were magical death muffins.

Footsteps echoed along the hall and Silvanya entered, looking rested and much calmer than a few hours ago. She wore a pair of ripped skinny jeans and a light knitted jumper—both courtesy of *my* closet seeing as Stephanie would have been too short to have anything to fit the slim, tall elf.

Her silvery hair though, was half hidden by a multi-colored, knitted hat—this one actually belonging to Steph—a few random tendrils escaping and framing her face.

Despite the relaxed attire, Silvanya still looked pretty much the regal princess that she was.

The princess now frowned as she glanced at the untouched muffins. "Are you not hungry?" she leaned over and grabbed a muffin, and began peeling back the blue polka-dotted paper.

How did I not know we owned such things as blue-polka-dotted paper cups?

Slightly relieved—although I wouldn't admit it if anyone asked—I reached for a muffin, wondering again when I'd turned into a pitiful lump of paranoia.

"Did you make these?" I asked as she popped a chunk of fluffy sponge into her mouth.

She nodded, silvery locks swaying. "We don't sleep much, so I had to find something to do. What bad manners I have," she spoke through her mouthful and gave me a sheepish smile. Swallowing hard, she wiped crumbs from her mouth and laughed. "Back home the ingredients are . . . slightly different."

We settled into a chat about baking ingredients, which for some strange reason led into a conversation on the difference between politics and sexism in the EarthWorld vs Kil'rith.

I was struggling to remain focused on the conversation, and a few minutes in, I got to my feet and smiled apologetically. "I'm really sorry I'm a little distracted. I'm expecting a message."

Slipping my phone from my jeans pocket I skimmed Natasha's texted response.

My place in twenty. We go together.

She certainly wasn't giving me much of a choice. The only consolation was she already knew about the poltergeist. I tucked my phone back into my pocket and lifted my gaze to meet Silvanya's.

I gave her a sympathetic smile, probably not enough but it was all I could offer her at this point. "I know the waiting is hard, but Elise will make a move soon. She's likely pissed at losing you, and she's not one to make decisions out of passion."

"Yes, she is a cold-hearted one." Silvanya's voice dripped ice, no doubt far colder than Elise Garner's frigid heart.

"Which would work in our favor. Cold-hearted means planned and deliberate. Which also means predictable."

Silvanya leaned against the kitchen counter behind her and wrapped her long arms around her body, as if trying to give herself the comfort she desperately needed. "I apologize if I seem . . . ungrateful. I'm worried about my father. About what she will do to him when she finally makes her move."

She pushed away from the counter and began to scrape crumbs off the table, letting them fall into the palm of her hand. Then she straightened. "Thank you for taking the time to reassure me. I hope I haven't kept you too long."

We said our goodbyes and I headed out, leaving her at the kitchen sink, staring out the window with her cupped palm still filled with muffin crumbs.

CHAPTER 31

I jumped straight to Natasha's place, arriving on her porch just as she walked out of her door.

Today her expression was somber and though I wanted to ask her what was up, we both had other things to think of.

She straightened her spine and met my eyes. "I don't know how smart this is . . . meeting him so far away from home turf."

I pursed my lips. "Yeah, but we don't really have much choice though."

She gave me a dirty look.

"*I* don't have much choice, you know. This is my last resort. Otherwise, *you* are going to have to upgrade from witch to necromancer so that I may survive this."

Natasha's lip curled and she gave a delicate shudder. "Thanks, but no thanks."

I hid a smile and patted my satchel where the printed copies of the Chinese script lay. "Right, then let's get going. The sooner we get there the sooner we get it done." I gave Natasha my elbow. "Now, where are we going?"

Natasha gave me the location and I did a quick search on my

phone's GPS for coordinates and a feel for the place. A little hard with miles and miles of sand.

Still, I projected first, arriving at the edge of the Sahara Desert where the sand bled across into Morocco. A quick confirmation of location was all it took to identify a presence that made my stomach turn.

I returned to my body and completed a good reproduction of Natasha's shudder. "I've said it before, and I will say it again . . . sorcerers make me sick to my stomach."

Natasha shook her head in warning. "What if he hears you?"

"How the hell would he hear me from all the way across the world?"

Natasha sighed. "You were near enough to him, Mel. He could very easily have locked onto your essence and traveled back with you."

"Shit. I didn't think of that." I was surprised that she'd suggested the possibility. Especially since I'd always believed my presence in the ether, and while projecting, was undetectable.

Until my most recent trip to find Samuel, of course.

I heaved a sigh and straightened my shoulders, steeling myself for the possibility of failure before we'd even begun. "It is what it is. *If* he heard, I'll beg for forgiveness."

Natasha squeezed my arm and I teleported us to the Sahara.

～

We arrived under an angry sun, and onto sand that burned right through the bottoms of our shoes. It took only a moment to find the sorcerer, who until now still remained nameless.

He stood on the summit of a sand dune to our left about fifty yards away, watching us. A wide-brimmed Texan hat cast convenient shadows, obscuring his features.

We began to walk along the dunes, scrambling to get to the ridge so it would be easier to get to him.

"What's his name?"

"Huh?" asked Natasha, a little distracted as she sank into the sand and had to dig her foot out before she stepped up beside me.

I kept my eyes focused on him. "What's his name," I asked out of the side of my mouth.

"Oh. Right," she looked up at the sorcerer. "His name is Saito."

"Just Saito?" I eyed her.

"Just Saito," she said softly. "There is power in a name. He believes his identity gives him power so he keeps that name to himself."

"Puts him at an unfair advantage, wouldn't you say?"

Natasha snorted. "He owes *me*. And he doesn't know who *you* are."

"Okay, then," I said softly and concentrated on putting one foot in front of the other.

But the heat was unbearable.

Wait a second.

I was a teleporter for crying out loud.

"Maybe I should just jump us there."

"No," Natasha barked the word out, unusually harsh for her normally calm and serene demeanor.

"Why not?" I was running out of breath, the heat clawing its way into my lungs while the sun scorched my skin and baked the top of my head.

"Because you don't want to expose the essence of your power to him. Most sorcerers have perfected the art of using the powers of other mages to boost their own."

I understood what she meant. Sorcerers fed off the powers of others, whether they were mages or supernaturals. I had to hope that Saito was not going to suck me dry before I got the chance to ask for the protection spells. I had it bad enough with my poltergeist who was again strangely reluctant to make his presence known.

The trek to the sorcerer was inelegant, sweaty, and damned tiring. By the time we reached within ten feet of him, both Natasha and I were exhausted, sweat-drenched clothing sticking to our bodies, while he remained calm and dry as if cocooned in a bubble of cool air.

Which he very probably was.

I hid my disgust and straightened in front of him.

His lips curled into an interesting smile as he scanned the two of us, head to toe then back up her again. His slim amber eyes sparkled, amused at our exertions, at our red-faces, and wet brows.

"I apologize for the difficulty of this trip, and the inconvenient location," he waved a hand around him, "In any other situation I might be amused." His expression said otherwise.

He moved aside, and I caught a glimpse of the dunes beyond him. My eyes widened at the sight of the undulating landscape—golden sands shimmering with heat, littered with hundreds of bread-loaf shaped rock formations.

I hid my surprise—and amazement as I'd never seen anything like it in my life—and met the sorcerer's gaze.

"Thank you for meeting us." My voice faded in the heat of the heated air.

His fiery eyes shuttered as he looked from me to Natasha, a frown creasing his forehead. "I am here only because I owe the *Witch* a favor." He rolled his shoulders and straightened, placing his hands behind his back. He turned his head slowly to look at my face, the disdain clear in his eyes. "What is it that *you* want?"

I hesitated, then withdrew the envelope of printouts. I handed it over to the sorcerer. "I need to create the magic that uses these glyphs."

He took the envelope and slid a finger beneath the flap. He tipped the printouts onto his palm and then flicked through the stack, his face an inscrutable mask. As last, he slipped them back into the envelope and looked up at me.

"What makes you think I will have anything to do with this type of magic?" He let go of the envelope and put his hands back behind him. The envelope floated in the air in front of him.

Okay, so he liked showmanship.

I glanced at Natasha, but I didn't want her to get involved. Yes, she'd called in a favor for me, but the request—and the responsibility attached to it—was mine alone.

I took a deep breath and said, "I was told that you would have the kind of power required to imbue these symbols with the magic I need."

Saito lifted a brow. "This is strong magic. I don't believe you know what you are talking about."

He shifted to stare off over my shoulder into the distance, dismissing me with a mere flick of his eyelids. Inhaling slowly, I said, "The person who sent me said specifically that you would have the power to help me."

He shrugged. "Rather presumptuous of him don't you think?" Saito shifted to face us again, his eyes narrowing. "I am losing my patience. Is this why you brought me here, *witch*?" he gave Natasha a sneering glare, "to be manipulated by a girl whose life-force is fading. Why would you want me to waste my time on *her*?"

I shook my head, clearing my throat to draw his attention back to me. "That's the very reason I'm here. I was told I needed to find the right sorcerer who'd be able to help me to make the wards work."

Saito shrugged again, his lack of interest clear. "You have wasted my time."

As he turned to leave, I took two steps toward him and tried to grab a hold of his arm. I'd been so upset—or too tired or drained—that I hadn't sensed the field of magic that surrounded him.

As I went flying into the air, I cursed my carelessness. I hit the dunes and was grateful that, though hard-packed, the desert sand had absorbed the impact and cushioned my landing.

I scrambled to my feet and glanced over at Saito. Had I blinked, I would have missed the subtle rising of his forefinger, like a conductor commanding an orchestra.

I frowned and glanced over at Natasha who was staring at the sorcerer, her expression filled with suspicion.

The atmosphere grew heavy, and the sound rumbled around us as if the air itself was about to come alive.

"Shit," yelled Natasha. She leaned over and grabbed hold of my arm. "Run," she screamed, tugging me along as she ran pell-mell down the side of the dune in the direction of the rock-breadloaf forest.

"What's going on?" I shouted as she dashed for the nearest of the rock formations.

"Get up there," her voice reached out and slapped me with its urgency—and with the fear filling every syllable—giving my feet a boost of both determination and magic.

I ran, my feet skidding, sinking deeper as the sand began undulating beneath my shoes. Holes appeared on the dunes, sand dripping into unseen depths.

I no longer cared that the sun burned my skin, that my clothes were soaked, that my head burned as if it were aflame.

No.

Not one of those things were as important as the fact that the very ground beneath my feet was coming apart and would soon swallow me whole if I didn't get my sorry ass up onto the nearest bread-loaf rock.

Scrambling, I threw myself forward, my body flying in an arc. My fingers grazed the rough surface of the rock and a sharp stabbing pain shot through two fingernails.

Just great.

Not that I was a manicure type of girl. It just hurt like a bitch.

I was tempted to teleport to the top of the nearest rock, but Natasha's warning rang in my head.

So I was forced to use mere human ability, which was second rate at best.

I jumped again, trying to grab hold of a narrow ledge of stone jutting out near the top of the rock.

I would have made it.

Had it not been for the rope wrapped around my ankle.

I kicked my foot trying to free myself of the rope, but it only grew tighter. I held on, desperately clinging to the rock and craned my neck to look over my shoulder at the rope.

Rope?

Not a rope.

A monster.

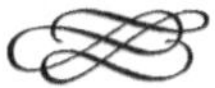

CHAPTER 32

The creature that held me in its grip was as far from a rope as was possible.

A thick, black and very hairy leg curled around my ankle, and I shuddered, forcing myself to focus on climbing despite the creature holding onto me.

The more I pulled, the stronger the monster's grip became and I struggled to hold onto the rock, bloodied fingernails making the surface slick.

"Mel?" Natasha yelled, her voice frantic. I turned my head to face her, suddenly afraid that she may also be under attack.

Thankfully, the creature had left her alone, and she was currently kneeling so far out on the edge of her rock that I half expected her to fall any second.

She glared at the undulating sand below me, and as I turned my attention to the movement, the golden grains revealed a momentary glimpse of a great glossy eyeball, then hid the creature from view.

Glancing back at Natasha, and at the look of determination twisting her features, I got a very, very bad feeling.

When she scrambled to her feet I yelled, "No. Don't. I'll be fine."

Natasha paused, staring from me to the thing wrapped around my leg, and then to Saito. "What the hell is this for?" she screamed at him. "Why are you doing this?"

Why, indeed?

The man was a few cards short of a full deck to behave so randomly when he'd agreed to the meet in the first place. He hadn't even heard me out properly.

Asshole.

My fingers slipped and I screamed as I slid down the rock face, certain I was going to fall into the sand and be consumed by the unseen monster. My fingers struck stone and I grabbed on for dear life, glancing up to find out what had stopped my fall.

An uneven ledge that rimmed the stone almost halfway down.

Halfway down?

Not good.

That meant I was far too close to the monster for my liking.

I glanced back down and this time, when I studied the thing gripping my leg, my eyes widened. The limb looked like an octopus tentacle, yet was covered in glistening obsidian skin and spiky black hair that glinted as if eager to plunge into my skin.

A scraping sound drew my attention from my predator and I snapped my gaze at Natasha.

My jaw dropped.

Natasha was using her magic to pull the stone off the ground, even after she'd said not to use any magical abilities.

But given that she was only using a minor levitational power, which the sorcerer no doubt already possessed, she wouldn't attract his attention.

Smart witch.

Unfortunately, the sorcerer turned out to be much stronger. A gust of wind slammed into Natasha, sending her and her rock hurtling into the air. The rock smashed into a nearby formation, with a hollow explosion, chunks of stone cascading to the ground from the impact.

Natasha, at the very edge of the formation, narrowly escaped being flattened like a pancake between the two rocks.

The sand below me boiled and something dark and immensely large surged upward toward me. It flew into the air, taking me with it, and as it leaped over the stones it swung me by the leg like a rag doll.

Natasha screamed out my name, and I rolled my eyes.

"Calling me won't help. Get him to stop this shit!"

I'd had enough.

From twenty feet away, I screamed out at the top of my lungs. "Darius sent me."

I'd been reluctant to reveal any details to the sorcerer, especially since I hadn't told Natasha about the ancient, but injuring my friend was enough reason to spill the secret.

And it worked.

My multi-limbed ride turned in a wide circle and used the tops of the rock formations to return me to Natasha. It dropped me beside the witch, who was standing hunched over vibrating with fury, blood streaming from a gash in her head, and cradling her left arm, which hung limply at her side.

Saito floated across to us, his expression dark. "What did you say?"

I huffed, eyeing the octopus-creature as it made its way down from the rocks and landed beside its master. All those glistening legs made me shudder.

"I said . . . Darius said you would help me. Now please, help already so we can all go home with our bodies still intact." I glared at him, my intent clear enough, although I suspected that though impressed with my mention of the ancient, he was convinced I'd never be able to take him.

Saito flicked a finger at his multi-legged pet. As it drew closer I made out details that wouldn't be easy to forget.

It looked like the lovechild of an octopus and a pit of snakes. Saito grunted, drawing my attention away from the hideous monstrosity. "I don't believe that the Ancient Darius would bother with the likes of you."

I shrugged. "You're welcome to your opinion." I folded my arms. "I can wait here if you'd like to pop over and ask him." I narrowed my eyes, watching him, my expression hard. I'd lost all patience with him and he wasn't blind to it.

As he considered his options—not that there really were any—I studied the black rounded head of the creature. The octo-spider's face was strangely human, if you ignored the living beard of tentacles hanging from its chin.

Only uglier.

"Very well." Saito flicked a finger and the envelope—which had been floating at his side all this time—rode the air toward him. He made a show of grabbing it from the air and opening it again.

After scanning the contents, a page at a time, he glanced up, "Why didn't you say so in the first place?"

I fumed silently, sharing a heated glare with Natasha who was busy dabbing at the cut on her temple with her sleeve.

Inhaling deeply, with the hope of calming myself, I said, "Can you do it?"

"Of course, I can."

That was all he said, leaving me with the desire to rush over to him and punch him in the gut.

Violent much, Mel.

"How long?" I bit the two words out, attempting to keep my tone neutral. I ended up sounding cold.

I didn't care.

He offered me a smile. He'd been pushed into a corner and he didn't like it. Worse, he'd acted like an arsehole before discovering my request came from a much higher level than a mere half-dead mage.

He sighed. "I suppose we ought to retire to much more comfortable surroundings."

A bit late, don't you think?

I glanced at Natasha's arm. "We need medical attention, thanks to your overzealous pet squid."

Saito glanced over, eyes widening at the sight of Natasha's broken arm. I couldn't believe that he'd had no idea of her injury, but if he wanted to pretend I didn't really care as long as he gave me the wards.

He floated closer and stopped a few feet from us. Raising a hand, he gestured in our direction and I fought against flinching.

Natasha let out a soft breath, lifting her—so recently injured—hand to shoulder length. Her expression made me smile.

More murderous than grateful.

"Do that again Saito, and I will not be held responsible for what I do to you."

That surprised me, but all the sorcerer did was give her a slow nod, as if conceding and agreeing.

It made me wonder which of the two was the stronger adversary.

Then he turned to me and said, "Let me not waste any more of your time."

He reached into the air in front of him, pulled a string of small pieces of red-painted wood, and tossed it so it spun in a slow circle. He muttered words I didn't recognize, words that hit me with harsh pulsating beats of energy, as if he was pounding his power into the wood.

As they spun I began to count them absently, my mind bouncing off what Saito was saying or doing.

I frowned and looked at Natasha who leaned over to whisper, "A magical ward. Protects his spell from being heard out loud."

"Guy has trust issues," I muttered watching the spinning charms.

Eight in all, they began to glow and tumble. From the corner of my eye I saw the flash of a red tail as the sorcerer shed his cape and ten-gallon and emerged fully into the sunlight.

I sucked in a shocked breath.

I'm not entirely sure what I'd expected him to look like, but this magically perfect blend of human and fox was so attractive I found my eyebrows rising in surprise.

"He's . . . "

"Hot?" asked Natasha, the corner of her mouth curling.

I let out a muffled snort. "For a canine."

She choked on a laugh but I was no longer paying attention. Even the good looks of an arsehole of a sorcerer weren't able to distract me from my own personal haunting.

Thankfully, I didn't need to say anything further. The string of wooden beads stopped spinning and as they ceased their tumbling, my eyes widened. He'd formed each piece of wood into a magical glyph, copying every one of the drawings and forming a string of quite cute charms.

Saito flicked a hand out and the charms floated toward me.

"You must keep them all on your person at all times. They work in concert with each other. While you wear them, you will be protected from the possession. But be aware that the spell-caster, the person responsible for sending this pestilence to you, will become aware of its sudden ineffectiveness soon enough. And he will most likely strengthen the spell. Should that happen, you may find me again to increase the power."

"Why not increased the power now?"

"Because long periods of exposure to the magic can kill you."

Sounds like I'm damned if I do and damned if I don't.

Thankfully, I didn't say it out loud. Besides, any reprieve from the poltergeist would be good.

I wound the charms around my wrist to form a chunky bracelet and looked up at the sorcerer. "Thank you," I said, grateful that he'd delivered. I was about to ask about payment when he lifted a hand and cut me off.

"You were sent by the Ancients. I do not require payment in their service."

I glanced at Natasha who looked about as surprised as I felt.

Neither of us got to ask him any further questions. He floated away, back to his dune, then settled onto the sand.

His dark eyes settled on Natasha's. "Witch." He inclined his head and gave her a cool smile. "Until next time."

Then he disappeared, leaving us alone with his octopus-spider pet.

I took one look at the creature as it gathered itself into a huddle, preparing to leap, and grabbed hold of Natasha's hand.

"We need to get the hell out of here."

CHAPTER 33

We arrived on Natasha's doorstep so fast that neither of us were able to stop our momentum, and ended up falling onto the floor in a tangle of limbs.

"Bastard," snapped Natasha as she got to her feet and dusted herself off.

I didn't point out that dusting her clothing was completely irrelevant since her shirt was covered in bloodstains, and torn in two places from the jagged edges of the stones.

I stood and stared at the charms, wondering if he'd really did as promised.

Natasha must have noticed the focus of my concentration. "Don't worry. He's a dick but he's true to his word."

I glanced up at her and gave her a half smile.

One she didn't return.

Uh-oh.

She was angry, yes, but worse was her expression, filled with hurt and anger.

"Natasha . . . I—"

She lifted her hand as imperiously as Saito had. "I don't need an explanation."

My mouth hung open, emotions warring within me. Do I force an apology on her now, or do I wait until she'd calmed down? Though an outwardly calm person, Natasha possessed a deep well-spring of emotion which usually fed her magic.

Now, her body sent waves of hurt and anger my way.

"I would have told you—"

Natasha turned and walked to the front door. She opened it, her back stiff, her fingers tight. On the threshold she turned to look over her shoulder at me. "Whatever you hoped to achieve .. . just be careful of the methods you use to obtain it."

I couldn't stand the hurt in her eyes. "Darius said—"

She turned to face me, her silvery eyes dark gray and iridescent. "I understand," she shrugged, "and perhaps I might have made the same call given the circumstances." She sighed and opened the door, beckoning me inside.

The shadows beneath her eyes screamed weariness—she'd be feeling worse than I was, having had her body pulverized. Even though Saito had healed her broken arm, she'd need time to rest before she was back to her usual self.

I was about to accept her invitation—even if just as a means to smooth things over—when my phone buzzed. A quick glance showed Steph's name and the word *Urgent!* blinking in green.

I glanced up at Natasha, my apology ready. But she smiled and waved me off. The hurt was still evident in her eyes but I had some hope we could get over this. I had to believe that considering I was losing people every side I turned.

I should have trusted her, but Darius had expected my confidence.

He'd specifically said to tell nobody.

And nobody included Natasha, no matter how close I was to her.

That she felt hurt by my omission, was both unavoidable and unfortunate. There was nothing I could do apart from apologize and explain.

My stomach twisted as I entertained—for the briefest moment—the possibility that she may never forgive me.

The phone buzzed again, this time *Urgent* came with four exclamation marks.

Sighing, I gave Natasha a small wave and jumped straight home.

~

"Is that you Mel?" she yelled.

I hurried up the stairs, shrugging out of my jacket. The inner lining was drenched with sweat and I was sure there was no saving it.

I'd have to throw it out.

Taking care to watch where I was going, I reached the top of the stairs, the clinking of my new wrist bling reminded me that the likelihood of a replay of the stairway-to-pain incident was very low.

I headed up to the comms room, making a face as I peeled my sodden shirt from my back. I needed a shower so badly.

The door to the comms room was ajar and I slipped inside to see both Erik and Steph staring up at the giant monitor.

"What's going on?"

Erik turned to look at me for a brief second. "The motion sensor finally picked up movement that led to something incriminating. We've got a recording." He'd already turned his attention back to the monitor as he spoke.

I hurried closer, and wasn't surprised to see Elise on the screen. She was standing over Raulfir, face contorted with fury.

"I guess she found out she's lost Silvanya. Certainly took her long enough to come to him."

Steph snorted. "Yeah, and she does not look happy."

Erik shook his head. "It's no joke. You do *not* know what my mother is like when she's on the warpath."

211

I suspected that Erik was concerned for Raulfir and turned my attention back to the screen. Elise appeared to be shouting instructions at the elf king, who was currently staring at her, shaking his head violently. The man did know how to act. You would never tell from his horrified expression that he *knew* that his daughter was safe.

"Do we not have sound on this?" I asked, annoyed that I couldn't hear what was being said.

Erik nodded. "There was some kind of a glitch in the feed, but the sound will be back."

Before I could ask him if he'd already seen the entire video, the sound returned and Elise's voice echoed through the speakers.

"I don't have time to waste. With your daughter gone, I'm afraid *you* are going to have to pick up on the slack. If you don't keep up with my schedule, I'll be forced to return to Kil'rith realm and retrieve more of your family."

The smile on Elise's face was cold, completely emotionless and downright scary.

Raulfir shook his head. "My daughter and I are the only two people in my realm able to produce these diamonds. The talent is extremely rare. You know this."

Elise shook her head. "I hardly see that as my problem. If your family is unable to produce the diamonds, it won't take much to get rid of the lot of them. Don't elves die in a burst of bright white light, leaving behind not a single trace?"

I was horrified that she would even think of such a thing, but again, I was not surprised. The only problem with her plan was Raulfir wasn't about to give in to her.

"And don't think for a moment that I believe only two of you have the power. I'll level Kil'rith looking for more Agamas Elves if I have to."

Raulfir's face paled. He took a halting breath. "Okay. Very well. I will do whatever you ask. Just leave my people alone."

When Elise moved around Raulfir, her hand came into view—she held something long and metallic within her fist.

The metal glowed with a subdued red light, and my stomach tightened. I'd seen such a weapon, one used by police and law enforcement agencies to subdue rioters.

With one marked difference. Its adaptation from its original purpose, to a tool used across various supernatural races to exact abuse.

A tweak here and there, and the weapon moved from an electrically-charged baton, to a branding iron. Every blow contained a blast of electricity, which included a deadly burn that seared through two layers of skin and sometimes reached bone depending on the force used.

From what I'd seen of Raulfir's arm, Elise had already taken advantage of him.

She raised the baton and slammed it down on his back. His scream echoed around the room and the hair on the nape of my neck stood on end. Instinctively, I scanned the room, relieved that Silvanya was not here to witness this horror.

Thankfully, Elise kept her torture to a single instance, and stood back to glare at Raulfir. "I can keep going all day. Tell me your decision and I can end this."

Raulfir nodded, almost sobbing as he gasped for air. "I'll do it. I'll do it. I'll do whatever it is you want, just as long as you leave my family out of this."

She smiled, a triumphant grin, more demonic than satisfied. "Very well, now get to work."

She took a few steps back and leaned against the wall watching Raulfir.

Waiting.

The elf shifted position, just enough for me to catch a glimpse of a large container of sand that had been placed in front of his feet.

I hid a wince.

I'd had just about enough sand to last me a lifetime.

Suppressing a shudder, I focused on the elf king. He gazed down at the sand and pointed his long elegant fingers toward it. Taking a deep breath, he exhaled slowly and as the air passed out of his lungs lightning shot from his fingers, white and eye-wateringly bright.

It hit the sand and exploded, the entire room filling with light. Elise had been smart enough to bring shades with her, which in turn was evidence enough that this wasn't her first rodeo.

As Raulfir sat back to reveal his handiwork, Elise smiled and stepped forward. She rummaged within the grains of sand and withdrew a handful of glittering diamonds.

I let out a shallow breath and relaxed, but only for a moment. The rest of the tape was pretty much the same, as Elise stood watching and the elf continued to send lightning into the sand and give her what she wanted.

The process very much resembled the formation of fulgurites in our earthly plane where lightning struck sand and created strangely-shaped crystals.

I'd never known that such a strike could create diamonds of such purity that people from across the world would bid astronomical amounts to buy them.

It was enough for a girl to lose faith in humanity.

As I watched the tape, steeling myself against the urge to jump straight to Hong Kong and knock Elise's lights out, my gut hardened with satisfaction.

With this tape, we had enough to put her away for the rest of her life. "I wonder why it took her this long to come see him?"

Erik shrugged. "Who knows. Probably her guards tried to hide their failure from her. Does it really matter?"

I stared at him. "Of course, it matters. We could be walking straight into a trap."

His eyebrows fluttered. "Yeah. I hadn't thought of that." His lips twisted into a sheepish smile and he turned back to the screen to stare at the image of his mother, frozen in time as she gloated over a handful of shimmering diamonds.

I looked over at Steph. "I need a copy of that. Stat."

She reached over to the table and handed me a small flash drive, giving me a wink. "Way ahead of you, sister."

I rolled my eyes, took the flash drive and said, "Tell Silvanya that I'll be back soon. Let's hope we're able to return her father to her very soon."

With the nod at Erik, I headed to my room. My shirt was soaked with perspiration, the wet fabric now growing colder after exposure to the air.

I needed a shower.

Stat.

After a quick and very uneventful shower, which also happened to be strange considering I didn't remove the chunky jewelry, I threw on jeans and a black shirt, staring at my daggers as I stowed them into my boots.

They were becoming a backup I seldom needed.

With a sigh, I teleported straight to the Elite Headquarters across town.

CHAPTER 34

I arrived in the front hall of the Elite Headquarters, disoriented for a moment at how homely the place looked. It was a suburban residence after all, converted into the base of operations for the newly-created investigative unit of the Supreme High Council.

The empty hall—the air heavy with the scent of furniture polish and an overpowering floral scent I failed to identify—was all that greeted me and I hesitated, shrugging my satchel higher up my shoulder, uncertain if I should yell for assistance, or exercise patience.

I chose patience under the assumption that being a supernatural agency, they'd have methods of detecting unannounced arrivals.

Man, you are so over-thinking things.

I waited in the front living room for a while, pacing lengths across the floor, wondering if this was the best—or more likely the worst—decision I've ever made. What if I endangered Raulfir's life with our plan? But what if Elise lashed out and hurt his family back in their realm?

But I had to do something about it. And Silvanya was relying on me. I had to believe we would get him out safely.

And the Elite was the only way I knew how.

A slim older woman hurried into the waiting room. She peered at me through black-rimmed glasses, giving me a sweet smile. "High Councilman Carter is ready to see you now. If you will follow me."

I hurried after her as she led me down the hall. The place was decorated beautifully, the hall shadowed, but not so dark that it would appear in a negative light. Small flickering lamps dotted the wood-paneled wall, throwing light onto old paintings, making the place seem comfortable rather than imposing.

The secretary drew to a stop and opened a door on our left, waving me inside. As soon as I entered, she closed the door behind me, and my stomach tightened.

I brushed the feeling away, annoyed that I'd fallen into a pattern of questioning everything and everyone.

There was just too much going on and I felt adrift.

An imposing pedestal desk took center stage in the small room, and even seemed to overshadow the floor-to-ceiling book-shelves on the left wall. A tall, thin man rose from his seat and reached out to shake my hand.

I hurried toward the table and leaned forward greeting him with a short firm shake before releasing his hand quickly.

His eyes grazed the new jewelry on my wrist, pausing briefly before straightening. "Mel Morgan. I'm High Councilman Michael Carter." He waved a hand, indicating one of the two armchairs flanking the front end of his desk. "I'm so glad you accepted our invitation."

I remained standing and shook my head. "Technically this is not about your invitation." I realized how abrupt that sounded and gave him a rueful smile. "I apologize if that seemed rude. It's just that time is of the essence in this particular situation and I'm certain you'd appreciate me getting to the point as soon as possible."

He frowned, but thankfully he didn't appear annoyed or angry. More curious than anything, for which I was grateful.

He gave me a short nod. "Well, what do you have for me. What is so urgent?" He made a rolling motion with his hand, encouraging me to speak.

I reached into my pocket, retrieved the flash drive and handed over to him. "That has everything that you'll need. But you have to move fast. I'm hoping you have the resources." No doubt he did, although it would be complacent not to ask.

A wave of dizziness rushed through me and I swayed, gripping onto the edge of the table, hoping I wouldn't pass out.

Thankfully, I didn't.

Instead, I sat gingerly on the edge of the closest armchair, and when I looked up his attention was already on the monitor of his laptop as he plugged in the flash drive. I wasn't sure whether it was a tactful move on his part, but I managed to relax and shake the dizziness off without him making a big fuss about it.

I respected the man already.

His laptop whirred and clicked, and he stiffened as he watched the video. I forced myself to remain still, and tried not to listen to the tape. I'd have preferred to not be in the room to listen to it again.

Grimacing, I tried to tune the sounds of Raulfir's pain out, and almost succeed until Carter's voice broke through.

"Where is this?" he asked already reaching for his phone. He paused as he waited for an answer, a scowl creasing his brow, his expression dark.

"Hong Kong." I rattled off the address of Elise Garner's Hong Kong headquarters.

I'd barely finished speaking when he began dialing. He made a quick call, alerting someone on the other end of the line that he needed an emergency Elite recon team to be dispatched in the next ten minutes.

When Carter put the phone down, I asked, "You didn't ask me who she was?"

He gave me a small, though humorless smile. "I know very well who Elise Garner is. She has been on our radar for a while but we have just not been able to prove our suspicions. Now, thanks to you, we have everything we need to put her away for a very long time." Both his tone and his way of speaking confirmed that he was possibly an immortal of some type.

Relieved, I sighed and sank back against the firm backrest of the armchair. "What can we do about her access to the Kil'rith?"

He nodded absently, as if he'd already begun to consider the problem. Then he took a breath. "Her portal key will be revoked, and because she would have obtained it through blood ritual, it will need to be severed *with* a blood ritual."

More blood magic?

I'd had about enough of blood magic.

CHAPTER 35

"How do we do this?" I shifted forward in my seat.

Carter shook his auburn head. "You don't need to worry about it." When I frowned he let out a soft chuckle. "All I mean is *you* don't need to do anything about it. We will contact High Priestess Kira of the DeathTalkers. It's quite likely that Elise obtained her seal through Lady Kira. We will ensure that her portal key will no longer work."

I pursed my lips and considered his reassurances. He had a plan so I wasn't complaining. It just felt strange suddenly being no longer involved. "What if she had other plans in place in case this kind of thing happens to her? What if she's got a team prepared to get her out as fast as she just got in?"

He shook his head. "Because of the severity of her crimes against all of the DarkWorld, the Ancients are involved. They want her punished. It's quite likely that even if someone speaks on her behalf, she will never see freedom again."

It sounded harsh, but it was exactly what she deserved. I spared a thought for Erik and what he would think about the situation.

I took a deep breath and for the first time in the last two

days I relaxed. When I lifted my gaze and met his eyes, he smiled. "I'm guessing today isn't the day to discuss joining the Elite?"

I laughed softly. "We might as well . . . since I'm here."

He nodded, a solemn look in his eye. "I will understand if you do decide that this is not the best time. By giving us this information you've helped us a great deal."

I smiled, taking advantage of that opening. "Well, maybe you can do me one more favor?"

He gave a short nod. "What is it?"

"The elf in the video. Do you know who he is?"

Another nod. "King Raulfir of Kil'rith, the Realm of the Elves."

I sighed, sad for what Raulfir had endured. "His daughter—Princess Silvanya—is at my house."

"So *you* retrieved her?"

I nodded. "With the help of Elise's son, Erik." Carter nodded, his face inscrutable.

His silence made me wonder if there was something he knew but wasn't telling. I decided to ignore my gut, figuring I was probably way too paranoid for my own good, what with all the crazy that was my life these days.

I sighed and leaned forward. "She's at my place. She wasn't too thrilled with the plan for him to help trap Elise, but she understood. She's waiting to see him again and I promised that it would be soon."

Carter nodded and I watched his expression. Still indecipherable. "Of course. We will ensure that his debrief is as short as possible. He will be reunited with his daughter very soon." Carter frowned and then shook a finger in my direction. "Come to think of it, we'd need to debrief her as well."

Though I'd expected it, my face fell. I didn't hide my disappointment, or my dissatisfaction, with the pace at which the Elite was working.

He must have read it all in my expression. "I understand your frustration. I promise we won't take too much of her time. We just need her side of the story."

He paused and looked back at the monitor which still bore the frozen image of Elise Garner. He gave the screen a nod, then shifted his gaze to me.

"And the boy's."

I didn't have a problem with that and I was pretty certain that Erik wouldn't have any issues with it either.

I gave Carter a nod. "How soon will you arrest her?"

He looked at his watch. "They've already been dispatched. The answer to that question is, as soon as recon returns with a report. We'll make our move once we have the plan in place."

I raised my eyebrows, surprised and impressed at the efficiency.

I fell silent for a few minutes, my thoughts now on the job offer. They had means, technology, manpower. All things that I lacked despite the connections I'd made through the years.

I shifted in my seat, still not entirely certain of my choice. "So if I do join your Elite team, how will that impact my work. I get requests to find missing people all the time. I have to admit I'm concerned. What if cases end up clashing . . . and I have to choose?"

Carter got to his feet and walked around the desk. He stopped in front of me, and sat on the edge of the desk. "I can assure you that cases will not clash. The moment you agree to come on board, we will give every one of *your* cases the utmost priority. And will treat them as if they are our own. You will have access to backup, medical intervention, and forensic diagnostics."

"So what do *you* get in return?" I asked.

This all sounded a bit too good to be true. I had to admit I'd give anything to have access to such a backup team, but not if the price was too high.

His lips curved into a warm smile. "We get Mel Morgan on our team. Your abilities will help us greatly. You are not the only one that receives requests to find missing people. The Supreme High Council believes that you will be a priceless addition to our team. As foreboding as it sounds, the future of the DarkWorld isn't as bright as we'd like to think. All we want is to be prepared for what comes."

He was definitely getting morbid, but I'd already had a run-in with Darius, and I was beginning to suspect Carter knew something about the Ancient's contact with me. But I didn't feel ready to discuss it with him. Not yet.

I smiled and got to my feet, hitching my satchel over my shoulder and holding onto the strap tightly. "I'm in, as long as we are able to coordinate and as long as our cases do not clash. If it ever comes to it, I *will* choose my own clients over those of the Elite."

He nodded, his expression kind and understanding. It wasn't often I came across an officer of any investigative agency who was this approachable. Again, it made me wonder if this was too good to be true.

And then I reminded myself that sometimes I did have to trust.

He got to his feet and walked past me, heading to the bookshelf. He rummaged inside one of the cupboards and handed me a flat box. "Your badge and the agency cellphone."

I nodded and deposited the box into my satchel without opening it. "Thank you. And I appreciate the agency's interest in me."

He smiled and guided me to the door. "My dear, you are far more important than you know. I only hope that when the time comes, you will be able to trust yourself to fulfill your potential."

I glanced at him, my brow furrowing.

A little cryptic for me.

But he ignored my questioning look and opened the door for me. We said our goodbyes and I headed to the front lounge before teleporting back into my kitchen.

I set my satchel on the table and withdrew the black box. Lifting the lid, I stared at the golden badge, and the brand-new cell phone. Were these two things going to be anchors around my neck?

I certainly hoped not.

Having agreed to the Elite's proposition, I began to wonder if they had approached anyone else. Certainly Kailin and Logan would be high on *my* list had I been given a choice.

And so would Saleem.

My heart tightened. I just couldn't get used to Logan's situation. I sent off a quick text to Kai, asking about Logan's condition and how she and Lily were doing.

Eyelids drooping, I longed for sleep, a little unsure now how long I'd been going without a good rest.

Rest would definitely be next on my list.

CHAPTER 36

Silvanya walked into the kitchen, her hair rumpled, her sweats and tee creased from sleep. I was glad to see that she'd been getting some rest. After an ordeal like hers she'd needed rest and recuperation.

"What news?" her voice was soft and gentle, yet held an unspoken command. She'd had enough and wanted it all to be done.

I was glad to be the bearer of good news. "The Supreme High Council has a team in play. Recon first and once they know the situation, they will head in and extract your father."

"And incarcerate that . . . woman." The vicious quality of the princess's voice didn't surprise me. In fact, it made me proud of her.

I nodded. "High Councilman Carter has assured me they'd hold her accountable for every bad thing she's ever done. I believe they already have a long list of crimes."

Silvanya inhaled deeply, as if all this time she'd not taken a peaceful breath. "How soon before my father is released?" Her eyes went to the staircase, half visible from the kitchen doorway.

I pursed my lips, wondering if she was concerned about Erik's feelings. "As long as all goes well with the extraction and then the debriefing, likely a day. They'll want you to come in for a debrief as well. Your testimony could likely be needed to put Elise away for good."

I felt a twinge of guilt that Erik was somewhere in the house and we were talking so blatantly about his mother.

Silvanya straightened her spine, for a split second seeming to grow taller and thinner. "I will tell them everything they need to know about Elise and more. The woman liked to talk." She leaned against the fridge and folded her arms. "I'm just worried that a woman of her financial means and her nefarious intentions would have plans in place to ensure she is exonerated quickly. Or at the very least, do some damage to my father's kingdom."

I nodded. The princess and I had been on the same line of thinking. "Carter assures me they will be negating the power of her portal key, ensuring she'd never be able to cross the veil again."

Silvanya's face tightened, the lines around her eyes deepening. "I would hope so. I'm very much of the mind to lobby for seclusion from the rest of the DarkWorld once I return home."

I stared at her. Seclusion was not a common practice, especially when the High Council still remained the highest form of authority across all the planes. She'd likely be able to lobby her own people, perhaps draw various Elvin kingdoms together to agree, but they'd still need approval from the High Council and the Ancients.

Her eyebrows arched, clearly seeing right through me. Not that it was a big leap to understand my point of view.

What she suggested was radical.

But I understood why she thought it a desirable option.

I was about to give her my undiluted opinion when my phone rang.

"Excuse me," I gave her an apologetic smile and she returned it with a slow nod. She pushed off the refrigerator and sauntered off, waving her fingers over her shoulder at me, the smile on her face telling me she understood.

"Hey, Kai," I said softly, worried that something else was going on. "How you all doing?"

"I'm doing okay. As well as can be expected. Anjelo's mom isn't taking it well. I have a feeling she's blaming me in a way."

"That's natural. She'll realize she's wrong pretty soon. Give her time." I spoke the words, hoping Kai would listen. "How's Lily?"

Kai sighed. "Lily is acting really strange. As if she'd accepted Anjelo's death even before we'd found him."

"I wondered the same thing," I said.

Another sigh.

"And Logan?"

"He's in some kind of coma. We've had him checked out and my dad—of all people—has taken over his care."

I laughed. "I did not see that coming."

"Me either," she said, a smile in her voice. "Let's hope he makes some progress."

"He'll be fine, Kai. Logan is strong." I stopped speaking as I realized that one person in this equation had no idea what was going on. "I'm just worried about Saleem."

Kai cleared her throat. "I was worried about that. You told me they'd planned on a mission to Mithras together?"

"Yeah. According to a message I got from Saleem they should have left before you called me about Logan."

"When did Saleem message you?"

"A few hours before you called." I was already beginning to see where she was headed.

"But Logan was missing for much longer than that," Kai said, regret in her voice.

I sighed now. "Saleem lied to me."

"He'd have his reasons, Mel."

I cleared my throat and shrugged off any feelings of hurt I had. Who was I to judge when I was lying to him myself?

And besides, he would have his reasons. I just hoped he'd made the right choice for the right reasons.

I focused on Kai, one more thing on my mind. "Tell me what happened with Storm?" I asked, still feeling numb because if his betrayal.

"Not until I know more. All I can tell you is we had a full-on battle with him, in which he took Logan in exchange for Lily's release." Kai inhaled sharply. "Storm isn't who he says he is. I'm so sorry Mel. I know you and he were close."

I nodded slowly, not liking that she'd refused to give me further details but understanding her position having been in the very same one with Natasha not too long ago.

"It's okay. I'll find out what's going on soon enough."

I was about to ring off when she asked, "Are you okay, Mel?"

"Me?" I let out a laugh. "I'm as well as can be expected."

"You just looked . . . drained. I'm worried."

I took a deep breath. "I'm fine. I promise. Just overdoing it a little bit but if you tell Saleem I will have to kill you."

Kai let out a soft laugh, and we both rang off with smiles on our faces.

A small pocket of happiness in a maelstrom of pain.

I stood in the study, reluctant to cross paths with anyone right now. I'd sent Steph a text bringing her up to speed, checked up on Erik who was in his room, face in his laptop, and had then come to hide out in my study.

I didn't want to see anyone. Not right now. Not when all my emotional baggage had just hit me full in the gut.

I dropped my satchel on the desk and began to pace, unable to remain still.

Now that Elise was well on her way to being arrested, I didn't need to focus on her case. Erik and Silvanya were both safe at my place, waiting to hear back from Carter on the progress of Elise's arrest.

At one point, I'd considered asking to be part of the raid, if only to get a feel for how the Elite operated, but my mind kept returning to the one thing that had broken my heart so badly that I'd tried to shut it out of my mind altogether.

Storm.

Storm and his betrayal.

I still could not come to terms with the fact that he'd betrayed Logan and Lily and Anjelo.

Everyone who knew Storm knew that he'd had a soft spot for Anjelo ever since he'd saved the boy's life a while ago.

I didn't recall the details but as the story went, Storm had found Anjelo shot by drug dealers when the kid had first come to the city.

Injured as he'd been, they'd needed medical attention from someone who knew paranormals existed so Storm had taken Anjelo to Kai at the hospital she'd been working at.

I couldn't imagine the depth of the betrayal that Kai was experiencing.

Storm had put me on to Tara the Fae MetalSinger who'd become one of my closest friends. What would she think when she found out about what Storm had done?

And Saleem? Did he know about Storm? Had he deliberately delayed telling me he'd spoken to Logan?

Or had he gone ahead and left for Mithras without Logan, wondering all along why his friend had abandoned him at the last moment?

Did Storm even understand how badly he'd hurt so many people? What the ramifications were for his actions?

I stiffened and came to a stop.

I knew what I had to do.

And to hell with the consequences.

I took a seat in the armchair that sat against the wall beside the door.

Closing my eyes, I sank into the back of the seat, reaching into the ether for Storm's feedback thread. The energy of his essence was strangely faint, as if dampened in some way; perhaps a magical ward of some kind.

Still, I grabbed onto the feedback and followed it directly to him, projecting into the room beside him. He couldn't tell that I was there, and I felt a little like a voyeur being in the same space with him without his knowledge.

He sat at a carved stone table, resting against the curved backrest of a marble seat. He wore leather sandals and a Roman dress that fell to his knees, red and gold painted armor covering the white silk.

His legs were half crossed, right ankle on the left knee, his body angled in an almost-sprawl, while he talked to the woman who sat primly before him.

"You do know this is a waste of time?" Storm said, a thin smile on his face.

His blond curls brushed his shoulders and his impossibly blue eyes were dark and brooding. His tone was arrogant and demanding as if she owed him her attention.

The dark-haired woman clearly didn't agree.

Her eyebrows lifted. "I don't see how this could be a waste of anyone's time. I'm very disappointed in you. And I think it's time you are held accountable for your actions."

He glared at her, dropping his foot and leaning forward to place his fists carefully on the table, the gold arm braces glinting in the sunlight filling the room.

"So what are you going to do this time?" his tone mocked her, "What can possibly be worse than being forced to live among those pitiful, pathetic creatures and pretend every day that you gave a fucking damn about them? *You* sent me to live among those pathetic mortals as some sort of insane penance. Don't be shocked that I tried to make the best of things."

The woman clicked her tongue then glided to her feet. "Now, now, son," she said as she walked to the wide doorway that led to a flagstone balcony.

A soft breeze played with the ringlets of curls framing her face but she stared out at the view—fruit trees and villas and bright blue skies. The smell of the ocean drifted into the room.

She wore a long Roman-style gown, her hair piled high on the top of her head and her face revealing both her age and her beauty, enhanced by the sunlight streaming inside.

She glanced over her shoulder at Storm. "That kind of language is uncalled for."

Storm laughed, the sound harsh and cruel, ripping jagged holes into my heart.

Wait. What?

Son?

Was this Storm's mother? And if so who was she?

My head throbbed as I considered possibilities, yet nothing that I could have come up with would have held a candle to the truth.

Storm pushed to his feet and walked to her. "Mother, I think I'm old enough to speak however I wish. Besides, it's your fault for sending me to live with those puny creatures."

The woman spun on her heel and stabbed a pointed finger into his chest. "Ares," she growled the name, the sound of it sending chills down my spine. "You brought this on yourself. Instead of contrition, you choose arrogance, instead of apologies, you sneer. Instead of building, you destroy."

"And how is that my fault?"

My attention to their conversation had waned the moment the woman had mentioned the name Ares. So Storm was the god Ares, banished to the EarthWorld as a form of punishment.

And the woman was Hera. The *goddess* Hera.

Crap.

I was so stunned I'd momentarily forgotten that I was supposed to be pissed off at him. Hurt by everything he'd done to us.

But, as I watched the mother and son—gods actually—discuss what his punishment will be for this second infraction, I realized that we really had meant nothing to Storm.

Ares.

Whoever the hell he was.

He'd been serving a penance, forced to be with us. Every moment had been a lie, a pretense. How then can such a person—

god or otherwise—be held accountable when they were not emotionally involved?

How did it even matter that he'd broken my heart? All of our hearts?

Would it make a difference now to demand a reason for what he'd done to us?

To me?

I stifled a gasp.

Could Storm have been the one behind my *tokolosje?*

Faced with the truth of who he was, I found myself considering the possibility.

Could he really have been the one to put that spell on me with the sole purpose being to end my life?

My heart rebelled against the thought, but my mind—watching the two gods discuss pathetic mortals—told me he was likely the spellcaster I'd been searching for.

And to think I'd suspected those closest to me, and I'd still never entertained that *he* could be the one.

I hovered there for a moment, a maelstrom of emotion filling me. Then, releasing a pained sigh, I returned to my body, deflated and frustrated.

Without a second thought I jumped to Natasha's front porch and knocked on her open door. She appeared inside the house, a pale form at the end of the hall as she hurried to me.

Her expression confirmed that she wasn't all that glad to see me.

Yeah, still mad at me.

I shrugged off the hurt and said, "I think I know who the spellcaster is." The angry set to her lips relaxed, replaced in an instant with a frown.

"Who?" she asked as she led me into her study.

I was tempted to let her guess, but my fury at Storm was bigger than anything I could control.

"Ares."

My hands shook and I had to curl my fingers into fists to stop the quaking.

"What?" she sat and I followed suit. Her brow furrowed in confusion and she tilted her head to study me, concern in her gaze.

She likely thought me nuts.

"The god Ares wanted to kill me."

Natasha shook her head. "Are you suffering from heatstroke? Should I test you for signs?"

"No, I assure you I am not losing my senses."

Natasha straightened, considering my accusation. "Okay, so why would Ares care about you? He's supposed to be confined to one of the circles of hell as punishment, so how he'd even be able to cast the spell I wouldn't know."

I folded my arms, more to press down on my aching heart than anything. "Because he was sent to our world as punishment. Life among the mortal pigs is a great enough punishment apparently."

Natasha opened her mouth to speak, then closed it again. "Wait . . . who are we talking about?"

I narrowed my eyes. "Think tall, blond, blue-eyed."

"No," she whispered, her eyes going wide.

"Yep," I said biting down on the side of my cheek to stop myself from crying.

Why the fuck did I want to cry anyway?

The truth was Storm was nothing to me. Had never been.

And will never be.

Natasha got to her feet. "So, if Storm—or Ares—put the spell on you, then we'd need *his* blood together with yours, to track the *Sangoma*."

I nodded. "Exactly what I was thinking."

"Want to go back for a blood sample?"

"Not particularly."

She rolled her eyes. "Want to get rid of your poltergeist?

I sighed. "Okay . . . fine." I got to my feet, forcing my muscles to hold me. Exhaustion was suddenly taking hold of me. "What do I do?"

On Natasha's instruction, I returned to Storm's side with a hypodermic needle, projecting first to ensure the coast was clear.

He stood on the balcony, the breeze tossing his golden curls every which way. He inhaled deeply, seeming to absorb the entire scene into himself, like a man long bereft of something he deeply needed.

I gritted my teeth, materialized right behind him and plunged the needle into his jugular. He froze, his muscles tightening against the needle, but it didn't stop me as I drew the blood while he was still too shocked to react.

He didn't even have the time to turn around.

I returned straight to Natasha's study, Storm's cry of frustration and anger ringing in my ears.

Handing her the half-filled syringe, needle still dripping Storm's blood, I said, "Are you sure he can't follow me here?"

Natasha reached for the needle and nodded, barely listening as she rummaged on her bookshelf and found a silver bowl.

She brought the bowl to the table and set it down carefully, as if it were made of glass.

She depressed the plunger and dripped half the contents into the bowl. Then she came to me, reaching for the tiny dagger that she kept on a chain around her neck. She handed it to me.

I didn't ask what she needed. This had been a blood spell after all.

I went to the bowl and paused, staring at the glistening red of Ares' life blood. Raising the little blade, I pressed it hard against the skin on the heel of my hand, taking some satisfaction in the pain of the blade cutting into my flesh.

I took a breath and watched the blood well from the wound,

then topped my hand over and squeezed a few more drops of blood onto Storm's—Ares'—all the while wondering how gods bled as red as us puny pathetic mortals did.

Natasha patted my arm and handed me a towel. I returned to my seat, pressing the cloth to the wound on my palm to stem the bleeding.

She withdrew a map of the world from the shelf behind her and spread it open on her desk holding it flat with two white crystals, a fat black candle and a carving of the ugliest gargoyle I'd ever seen.

Natasha turned to the bowl and straightened as if steeling herself against any emotion while touching Storm's blood.

She had to be hurting too.

Natasha dipped her finger into the blood, swishing it around until it mixed together. Then she drew out a dripping wet finger of blood and held it over the map.

The drop pooled at the tip of her finger, then grew larger and heavier until it fell.

But it defied the laws of gravity and descended to the map in a wide angle.

The drop hit the paper with a loud smack and both Natasha and I stared up at each other.

The droplet of blood completely covered the city of New Orleans.

Natasha let out a soft breath. "I suppose that makes some sort of weird sense."

"Just because voodoo is practiced in NOLA doesn't mean people there practice African Black Magic."

Natasha shrugged. "I can't possibly speculate about the current interest in this type of magic. It's said to be an extinct magic, but *you* are living proof that it isn't."

I sighed and sat back, pressing harder against the cut in my palm.

"You know what this means right?" she asked, her eyes dark with worry.

"Yeah, yeah. It means I need to go to New Orleans to find me a *Sangoma*."

CHAPTER 38

I woke surprisingly rested. When my head had hit the pillow a couple hours ago, I'd passed out almost instantly from sheer exhaustion.

I'd fallen onto my bed, fully clothed, exhausted both physically and mentally, my inability to work out a proper more regular routine still messing with my body clock.

It just didn't happen in my day.

And the last few days were a testament to that fact. Now I had a trip to New Orleans to plan.

Turning onto my side, I plumped up the pillow under my head and took a deep breath. Staring at my nightstand, I studied the items. A set of ancient daggers I hardly ever used, a little silver alarm clock I never lived by, a gleaming gold badge and brand new state-of-the-art cellphone I'd soon to be controlled by.

As I watched, the cellphone shifted half an inch toward the edge of the nightstand. It shivered, then shot over the edge.

Shit.

The phone fell and I lunged forward, the red bracelet of

warded beads chinking against each other as I grabbed it before it hit the wood floor and shattered into bits.

I was half on the bed, half off, my head upside down, hair hanging to the ground, cursing the seemingly powerless charm bracelet, one hand on the floor and one occupied by my new phone.

And then the cell phone rang.

Typical.

I answered it while still upside down, the blood rushing into my head.

Not good for nosebleeds.

Carter's voice vibrated in my ear as I slipped from the bed and landed on three limbs onto the floor. "Agent Morgan?"

"Sir?" I responded.

"Morgan, I have a confirmation from the team that King Raulfir was extracted safely. I thought you'd want to know."

I let out a sigh of relief knowing Silvanya would at last be at peace. Then I thought about Erik. "And Elise Garner?" I asked, keeping my voice down as I got to my feet and slid the daggers into my boots. I sat on the edge of the bed.

"Happy to report that she is in custody and will stand trial soon."

I nodded to myself. "Would you be asking anyone to stand as witness?"

"I don't believe so. The Ancients have their ways of ascertaining guilt without the need for anyone to endanger themselves by providing evidence against her."

"So you believe she could still be a danger to her son and to me?"

He cleared his throat, but I heard an odd hesitation in his voice. "I don't believe so, but I do think it pays to be careful."

"Okay. And what about Erik Garner? He's still with me." I was concerned about where Erik would go from here. "Without his mother running the family business, would Erik be required to head up the businesses?"

"Not until the investigation is completed. All Garner's assets and business activities have been frozen. But it shouldn't take too long to complete the investigation. The boy will have the business under his control soon enough." Carter's voice was suspiciously toneless.

What was he not telling me?

I cleared my throat. "I'm not sure he wants anything to do with the diamond part of it. Not from what he mentioned to me."

"Whatever his decision will be, we won't be liquidating anything. Not until he takes control and advises his wishes."

Sounded like Carter had things pretty much under control.

"Ok. And how long before Raulfir and Silvanya can go home?"

"King Raulfir will be debriefed soon and then released. We have no reason to hold him. I will have the team deliver him to your home as soon as we're done."

"And Silvanya's debrief?"

Carter cleared his throat. ". . . won't be necessary."

He sounded cheered by the fact and I didn't argue, certain that the princess would be only too happy to avoid interrogation of any kind.

I thanked Carter, glad he'd taken the time to get me up to speed. Ringing off, I got to my feet and headed to the bathroom to wash up.

The red, charm bracelet chinked on my wrist reminding me again the peace I'd hoped for had been somewhat received.

Somewhat. Just not enough.

The damned poltergeist had wanted to ruin my phone, and that he'd almost succeeded despite the wards pissed me off.

CHAPTER 39

Feeling a little better after brushing my hair, I pocketed my gun, phones and badge—so weird—and went search of Steph and our guests, who I found gathered in the living room eating popcorn and watching an old movie about a red-suited man with super speed.

I entered the study with a smile on my face bringing Silvanya to her feet in an instant.

"Do you have news?" she whispered, wringing her hands and she walked toward me.

I nodded. "Your father will be here soon and there won't be a need to debrief you."

The girl let out a cry of joy and threw her arms around me, almost squeezing the life out of me.

I hugged her and patted her on the back, meeting Steph's approving eyes as she watched from the sofa. Erik had gotten to his feet, and was watching from beside the sofa, an odd look in his eye.

Silvanya leaned closer and whispered words in my ear that chilled my blood, words I did not want to believe.

It must have been the shock on my face that gave it away. Erik stiffened, staring at me, his eyes darkening as he took a step toward a totally oblivious Steph.

Everything fell into slow motion as I watched Erik reach inside his jacket and withdraw two guns. Steph's eyes went wide as he moved to aim his right-hand gun at her.

Silvanya stepped to my side, aware now that something in the air had changed.

Erik's second weapon came up slowly, pointing straight at Silvanya, but even as I considered jumping her to safety I knew Steph would remain in danger.

Choices I could not make.

Erik's guns were rising, almost aimed and I could see every crease in his skin as his fingers curled around each of the triggers.

My limbs moved, muscle memory from years of training kicking in. Low at the knees, my fingers curled around each of my daggers.

Metal sang as the blades were slid from their sheaths.

My fingers gripped hilts tight and I wasn't even aware of having made a decision.

Only when the blade left my open palm did I register what I'd done.

A gunshot went off as the dagger slammed into Erik's chest, slicing between the ribs over his heart. Red bloomed around the blade where it had embedded itself into Erik's flesh, so deep that only an inch of it remained between his body and the hilt.

My heart stilled at the shock on his face.

His body began to vibrate as he attempted to phase away, but he was too late.

The blade had hit its mark.

The light fled from his eyes even as he glared at me, hatred clear in his eyes.

How had I been so wrong about him?

Erik fell, knees slamming into the ground. He teetered there for a few moments before falling onto his side and crashing into the coffee table, smashing it into pieces.

Both guns clattered to the floor beside his lifeless body as Steph sprang away from the sofa to come to me.

Her words were calm as she shushed me, whispering that I'd had no choice.

Her fingers pulled the second dagger from my grip, slowly uncurling each stiffened finger, rubbing my frozen hands between hers, cupping my cheeks.

Sounds buzzed, unrecognizable in my ear until the front door opened and suddenly I could hear with crystal clarity.

Mayhem.

That was the only word I could use to describe our living room over the next hour. The Elite team had arrived to deliver Raulfir, only to hear the gunshot and come rushing inside.

A part of me registered they'd broken through the magical wards—that shouldn't have happened.

When excruciating pain bloomed in my side, I looked down stunned as I watched blood stain my shirt. I'd been hit but I didn't care.

I'd been so wrong about Erik.

"Erik is the one who tortured me," Silvanya had whispered in my ear, "I was too afraid of him to tell you."

Had he been innocent, he wouldn't have understood the reason for my shocked expression. Nor would he have decided to shoot us in response.

"I'm so fucking over being betrayed."

I flinched as my words rang around the silent bedroom. I glanced at Steph snoring softly on the bed beside me. She'd insisted on keeping me company just in case and I wondered who needed the comfort more— her or me.

Raulfir and Silvanya had taken their leave. Erik's body had

been taken away. And a crime scene cleanup tech had taken care of the bloodstains on mom's old carpet.

Carter had come by to check up on me, and Steph had called to give Natasha an update.

Now the room echoed with silence.

Accusatory silence.

CHAPTER 40

*I*nhaling harshly, I slid from the bed careful not to wake Steph. I tiptoed downstairs to the kitchen, going through the motions of making tea.

Boil water, pour, steep, milk, sugar.

When I finally sipped it, I discovered I'd forgotten the teabag altogether.

I set the mug of milky water on the table and studied my phone. No call from Saleem.

Which reminded me I'd had no success with Samuel. And I had to tell Darius what had happened.

I grabbed my phone and placed a call to the ancient, giving him a brief update on everything that had happened including Erik's betrayal. I didn't talk about a certain god who'd laughed as he'd trampled our hearts.

Darius studied me for a moment, his eyes flicking to my arm. "Have the wards functioned in protecting you until the spirit is removed?"

I nodded and gave him a reassuring smile, but my voice would have clearly revealed my uncertainty. "It's been better. But I suspect I'd need time to recover so I'm strong enough."

"Have you tried to look for Samuel again?"

I shook my head. "There's been a lot going on, and my power for such an extensive tracking isn't strong enough. Not yet."

He nodded, his expression serious and worried. "I hope you don't do anything rash."

I frowned. "Regarding what?" I asked, already suspecting we'd moved on to another sore topic.

"You know what I'm talking about." He nodded, his expression inscrutable now. "Do not act without thinking it over first. Often such actions come back to haunt you."

I nodded and smiled, hiding the hurt in my eyes.

How had he sensed where my mind had been? He knew already that I'd planned on seeking out Storm again. I hadn't obtained the explanation I needed from him.

Darius laughed. "I can tell a lie when I see one, young lady."

I gave him an apologetic smile.

He leaned closer until his face filled the screen. "There is much that you will come to learn over time. You will need strength to face the adversity that will befall the DarkWorld. But you will not be alone."

I frowned and shook my head. "What-"

He lifted a hand to silence me. "Under your pillow, you will find a message. Read it with care, and treat the information with even more care." Then his image shrank as he moved away. "And now I must leave you. Know that I am always here for you, should you need me."

I'd barely given a nod in response when the screen went blank. Off balance, I straightened, frowning and wishing he'd be a little less cryptic.

Then I stiffened.

Under my pillow?

I hurried upstairs and tossed my pillow on the floor, revealing a brown paper envelope.

Inside was a single sheet of yellowed paper, a few paragraphs of scrawled cursive majestically occupying the center of the paper.

I used my cellphone torchlight to read the words.

In the Dark World, when the night is black,
When darkness looms, to swallow you whole,
A quintet of courage will bring forth hope,
And reach across the planes to save heart and soul
She who shreds the Veils and she who hunts the Demons,
She who mends Minds and she who speaks beyond the Grave,
And she who bears the face of all - these five shall be as one.
For they are the saviors of the DarkWorld, they are the Ni'amh...

What in the world did that mean?

I reread the words, frowning as I tried to identify the people the poem mention.

The one who shreds Veils was most likely me. The demon hunter could well be Kai. A mender of minds had to be a Mind-Melder and the only one of impressive power that I knew of was Darcy Graham.

The DeathTalker could be Nerina, but I couldn't be sure. The soft-spoken girl had never seemed much of a fighter to me.

And the wearer of faces? Probably a ShapeChanger like Cassandra Monteith.

What did it all mean?

And why us? What was so important about us that we'd be summoned together to form this group called the Ni'amh?

Whatever it was, there was no doubt we'd eventually find out. But for now, I had other things to think about.

Ari and Samuel were still lost to me. Both Drake and Saleem were gone, and I had no idea if they'd return.

And Storm, my mentor and guardian for so many years, had betrayed me.

Erik, the victim, had been the perpetrator, wanting to abduct Silvanya in order to keep the diamond production going after he took over his mother's business. Elise Garner had been right after all—her son was really after the family business.

And a witch doctor awaited me in New Orleans.

My heart needed healing, but who knew if I'd ever have time to fully recover.

Especially with a future that looked filled with dire predictions.

Whatever came my way, there was one thing I was damned sure about.

I didn't plan on taking anything lying down.

~TO BE CONTINUED~
Mel's Adventures continue in Demon Soul.

FREE STARTER LIBRARY - JOIN MY NEWSLETTER

Get the following titles FREE when you subscribe to my newsletter.

Tee's Newsletter

http://smarturl.it/TeesMailingList

ABOUT THE AUTHOR

I have been a writer from the time I was old enough to recognize that reading was a doorway into my imagination. Poetry was my first foray into the art of the written word. Books were my best friends, my escape, my haven. I am essentially a recluse but this part of my personality is impossible to practice given I have two teenage daughters, who are actually my friends, my tea-makers, my confidantes... I am blessed with a husband who has left me for golf. It's a fair trade as I have left him for writing. We are both passionate supporters of each other's loves – it works wonderfully...

My heart is currently broken in two. One half resides in South Africa where my old roots still remain, and my heart still longs for the endless beaches and the smell of moist soil after a summer downpour. My love for Ma Afrika will never fade. The other half of me has been transplanted to the Land of the Long White Cloud. The land of the Taniwha, beautiful Maraes, and volcanoes. The land of green, pure beauty that truly inspires. And because I am so torn between these two lands – I shall forever remain cross-eyed.

Stalk Tee here:
www.tgayer.com
tee@tgayer.com

facebook.com/TGAyerAuthor

twitter.com/TGAyerAuthor

bookbub.com/profile/t-g-ayer

9 780099 511253